Leah laid a protective hand on Joy's head.

"Patience and kindness are the keys to raising a special child," she told Caleb. "All children are gifts from God, but we believe a child such as Joy is one of His most cherished gifts."

Caleb's hands dropped to his sides. He looked…defeated. "I know what the Amish believe. That's why I'm here. The *only* reason I'm here."

She didn't understand. He tipped his head slightly. "The prodigal son has returned. You don't look happy to see me."

She wasn't. She didn't care if he knew it. He had changed a great deal in the past nine years. The wild, handsome Amish boy she had known had matured into a tall, rugged-looking man with a muscular frame and deeply tanned skin. He wore his dark hair cut short in the *Englisch* way, not in the bowl-cut style the men of her community wore.

Leah realized he was studying her, too. Watching her with hard, piercing gray eyes that gave away little of what he was thinking.

Books by Patricia Davids

PATRICIA DAVIDS

After thirty-five years as a nurse, Pat has hung up her stethoscope to become a full-time writer. She enjoys spending her new free time visiting her grandchildren, doing some long-overdue yard work and traveling to research her story locations. She resides in Wichita, Kansas. Pat always enjoys hearing from her readers. You can visit her on the web at www.patriciadavids.com.

Amish Christmas Joy
Patricia Davids

HARLEQUIN® LOVE INSPIRED®

Recycling programs for this product may not exist in your area.

™ LOVE INSPIRED BOOKS

ISBN-13: 978-0-373-87855-0

AMISH CHRISTMAS JOY

www.Harlequin.com

Printed in U.S.A.

Whosoever shall receive one of such children in my name, receiveth me: and whosoever shall receive me, receiveth not me, but him that sent me.
—*Mark* 9:37

This book is lovingly dedicated to the parents of special-needs children everywhere.

Chapter One

Loud pounding pulled Caleb Mast out of the first good night's sleep he'd had in a month. He squinted at the clock on his bedside table. Who was beating on his door at three-forty in the morning?

Staggering out of bed, he made his way through his condo. After four weeks on an oil platform in the Gulf, he was ready for some downtime. He'd stayed twice as long as his normal rotation to cover for an injured crewmate. The twelve- to thirteen-hour shifts seven days a week were tough. Lousy weather and a shorthanded crew made the extra two weeks a killer. All he wanted was to crawl back in bed.

If some of his crewmates were looking to celebrate on their first night in, they could have fun without him. He didn't do the party scene. Not since… He dismissed the thought without finishing it. He didn't look back. The pounding resumed.

He yanked open the front door. "If this building isn't on fire you're in trouble. What?"

A woman stood on his doorstep. She had a little girl beside her. Thunder rumbled in the distance. A fine mist was falling, scenting the air with rain and making a shim-

mering halo around the streetlamp across the roadway. A yellow hatchback with a dented door sat parked beneath it.

The woman pushed back her frizzy blond hair. "You're a hard man to find, Caleb."

The voice belonged to a bad memory from his past. "Valerie?"

She gave a halfhearted smile. "You remember my name. That's something."

Was she kidding? He had turned his life upside down, cut bone-deep family ties and moved halfway across the country with Valerie Perry. A year later, she left him a goodbye note with no forwarding address and an empty bank account. Now, after nearly nine years, she was back. Why?

There were dark circles under her eyes and a droop to her full lips. She was thin as a rail. Her once-thick brown hair was bleached a brittle white-blond. It made her look cheap. Even at this hour, she wore heavy eye makeup. She licked her dry, cracked lips.

He folded his arms over his chest. "What do you want?"

"You could pretend you're happy to see me."

"If you're here to repay the money you stole, then I'm thrilled."

She dropped her gaze. "I've come for…another reason."

"Mama, I'm tired," the girl whined. She peered at him through a mop of blond hair, straight and pale as wheat straw. He was stunned to see the characteristic round face, small upturned eyes and slightly flat nose that indicated she had Down syndrome.

His Amish mother had always told him such children were God's most precious gifts, sent to special families for a special purpose.

"I'm hungry. I wanna go home." The girl's speech was slow and halting. She hid her face against Valerie's leg.

"Hush. I'm talking," Valerie snapped.

Sympathy for the kid made Caleb take a step back from the door. October in Houston was balmy compared to the crisp autumn weather of his childhood home in Ohio, but the rain was picking up. "You want to come in?"

She steered the child past him into the living room. "Lie down on the sofa while we grown-ups talk."

Talk about what? What did they have to say to each other after so long? He should have shut the door in her face. She wouldn't be here if she didn't want something.

"But I'm hungry, Mama."

No matter what Val had done, the child deserved his kindness. "I've got some cold pizza and milk in the fridge. It's not much, but she's welcome to it."

Breakfast of champions. His Amish mother would be horrified to see him feeding a kid pizza at this time of the night. Then again, she'd be horrified by a lot in his current life.

The look the girl gave him was tired, fearful and hopeful all at the same time. He crouched to her level. "It's pepperoni pizza. Is that okay?"

She nodded once. He glanced at Valerie. "Would you like something? Coffee?"

"Sure." She followed him into the kitchen. He pulled a pizza box from the fridge, placed a slice on a paper plate and stuck it in the microwave.

Valerie took a seat at the glass-topped table in the corner. "Things are such a mess. I didn't know where else to go. My boyfriend kicked us out, the jerk. My mom died last month."

"I'm sorry." Caleb had never met her mother. He shot a look toward Valerie as he spooned grounds into the coffeepot. She had a tight grip on her purse. She bit the corner of her lip and looked everywhere but at him. When the microwave bell dinged, she almost jumped out of her chair.

He checked to make sure the slice wasn't too hot, then

carried it into the living room. Valerie's daughter was sitting upright on the sofa, struggling to keep her eyes open. He handed her the pizza. "I'll get your milk in a minute, okay?"

She snatched the plate from him and started tearing into the pizza. He went back to put a second slice in the microwave. Clearly, one wasn't going to be enough.

Valerie was on her feet, pacing the length of the room. "Mom's old man doesn't want the kid around anymore. Not that Joy is a problem. She's not. She's quiet as a mouse."

"Joy, is that her name?"

"Yeah, Joy Lynn."

"Nice." What else could he say?

"I thought you'd be married by now. I remember how much you wanted kids."

"I came close, but it didn't work out. She went back with her ex." And took her two kids with her. Another painful chapter of his life with a rotten ending. Parenthood didn't seem to be in the plan for him. The coffee finished dripping. He took a mug out of the cupboard and began to fill it.

Valerie sniffed and rubbed her nose with the back of her hand. "Joy is your daughter. I thought you should know."

He replaced the coffeepot with great care and set the mug down, amazed that he hadn't dropped either. "What?"

"I know I should have told you sooner, but she's your kid."

"I don't believe you." Val always twisted the truth.

"Joy, how old are you?" she asked over her shoulder.

"I'm eight, Mama."

"When is your birthday, honey?"

"You know that. December twenty-fifth. That is Christmas Day. Nana says I'm her Christmas Joy...only, she has gone to heaven, hasn't she?" Joy's voice faded away.

Valerie had left him in early summer. It was actually possible.

Unlike the last woman who claimed he fathered her babe.

He refused to think about that final, painful confrontation with his Amish family. He had to focus on the present problem. Gripping the edge of the counter, he glared at Valerie. "Is this some kind of joke?"

She took a step back. "No. Mom's death made me realize that Joy should get to know you. You're all the family she has left."

"She has you," he retorted, wondering what kind of mother she was. Hard to imagine the self-absorbed, party-all-night woman he'd known in that role. He glanced toward Joy in the living room and his heart skipped a beat. He had a daughter.

If Val was telling the truth, he'd missed eight precious years of his child's life. The knowledge made him ache inside. Why had Valerie kept this from him? He would have stood by her. She had to know that.

"Mama, can I have my milk now, please? I remembered to say please. I'm being good."

Valerie arched one thinly penciled eyebrow. "Can she have some milk, Caleb?"

He wouldn't get his hopes up. Valerie could be lying. It was nothing new for her. He yanked open the fridge, pulled out a carton and handed it to her.

She took it, filled a glass with milk and carried it into the other room. He moved to the doorway to watch.

"Here you go. Mama left her cigarettes in the car, sweetie. Will you be okay with your daddy while I go get them?"

Joy jerked upright. "I have a daddy?" The kid sounded as surprised as he was by the news.

"Yes, you do. His name is Caleb Mast."

"A real daddy?" Her wistful tone carried hope and wonder.

"Your real daddy," Valerie assured her.

Joy's eyes narrowed. She pulled back and glared at her mother. "Is he another uncle like Jimmy and Keith?"

"No. He's your father. You're going to love him."

"What if I don't?"

What if she didn't? He wasn't a puppy or a kitten, something a kid liked on sight. He scratched at the stubble on his cheek. He was an ex-Amish oil-rig roughneck with few manners and a job that took him away half the year. He wasn't anyone's idea of a daddy. He'd given up that dream.

He turned away to get the forgotten pizza from the microwave and heard the front door open and close. He carried the second slice to Joy. She smiled when she saw it and licked the milk mustache from her upper lip.

What if she is my daughter?

Did it change anything? He didn't know her. She didn't know him. How much bonding could happen in the short time he spent ashore? Besides, he was about to take a job on one of the rigs off the coast of Brazil. He stood next on the company list to transfer. He expected to get word to pack his bags any day. He'd be gone for a full year when the opening came through.

She finished the milk and handed him the plate with the glass. "I like pizza."

"No kidding."

"I like animal crackers the best. I eat all the elephants first." She rocked as she smiled.

Thunder rumbled, closer now. Her smile vanished. She glanced fearfully at the window. "I don't like thunder."

"Don't worry, it'll be gone soon."

She gave him a hard look. "Promise?"

"I promise."

"Can we have pizza tomorrow?"

Where would she be tomorrow? "You'll have to ask your mom."

"Okay." She yawned widely.

He might as well get her settled. He wasn't going to send her and her mother out into the storm. Valerie had a lot more explaining to do. He gathered the bedding and soon had Joy tucked up snugly on his sofa. She was asleep in less than a minute. He bent and brushed her hair back from her face.

A special child was given for a special reason. What reason could God have for sending Joy to him?

She was a sweet kid, but was she his sweet kid? There was testing for this kind of situation. He would insist on it. Val was up to something. He settled in his recliner and waited for her to return.

Three hours later, the storm had moved on. Morning sunlight crept in beneath the window shade. Caleb rose from the chair and opened the front door for the umpteenth time. Birds twittered in the dripping trees. The walkway and street out front were glistening wet and deserted.

Valerie hadn't come back.

He heard a noise behind him. Turning, he saw Joy standing beside the couch. "Where's my mama?"

"I wish I knew."

Fear darkened her eyes. "I want my mama."

"Hey, it's okay." He started toward her without a clue what to do next.

She backed away. "I gotta find her."

She darted around him and ran barefoot out the door toward the street, with Caleb close on her heels.

Leah Belier added a box of crayons to her basket as she shopped with her friend Joann Weaver in the small grocery store in the village of Hope Springs, Ohio.

"Are you taking up art in your spare time?" Joann asked with a grin.

"*Nee.* I noticed Emmy Chupp borrowing colors from the other students this afternoon. She loves to draw. I think she

has used up the ones her mother sent with her at the beginning of the school year. I decided to get her some more."

"For Christmas?"

"That's still four weeks away. She needs them now. I'll get her colored pencils as a Christmas gift."

"That's sweet of you. How is her father getting along? I heard he broke his leg."

"He hasn't been able to work at the lumberyard for several weeks. Honestly, I'm worried about the family. Emmy didn't bring any lunch today. She told me she forgot it at home."

"Knowing you, I expect she ate your lunch, and you went hungry."

Leah chuckled. "It wouldn't hurt me to miss a meal or two, but I always bring extra food just in case."

She had shared her ample sandwich with Emmy and made a mental note to check in on the family tomorrow. As the teacher at the local Amish school, Leah kept a close eye on all her students. She was in a better position than most to see where trouble was brewing.

A new box of twenty-four crayons would cheer the shy child who liked to draw. Leah added some peanut butter and jelly to her basket. A few extra groceries might come in handy with lunches. If it looked as if they needed more help, she would let Bishop Zook know. No man's family went hungry in their Amish community. Caring for one another was a duty, not a chore.

She carried her purchases to the front of the store. The *Englisch* owner, Mr. McGregor, ran her items over the scanner. A big bear of a man with thick, curly gray hair, a wide smile and a booming voice, he and his tiny wife were longtime fixtures in Hope Springs.

"Afternoon, ladies. I hope all of you plan to come to the Christmas parade. Since this is our first year, we want it

to be a success. My kids are building a float for the store. Should be grand."

"We are looking forward to it," Joann said.

"Mrs. Weaver, the printing job you did on the flyers for our dented-canned-goods sale was great. Lots of people came, not just the Amish."

Joann blushed. "Miller Press is happy to serve all those in our community, Amish and non-Amish alike. I will tell my husband you were pleased."

Joann and her new husband, Roman Weaver, both worked at his uncle's printing business.

"Good. Leah, my wife and I were just saying how much we're looking forward to your school Christmas program this year. Are the children getting excited?"

"Indeed they are. You and your wife are always welcome."

"My wife had the lights and decorations up the minute Thanksgiving was over, but it's watching your Amish students put on their plays and sing their songs so wonderfully that brings the true meaning of Christmas to my heart."

"I'm glad, for that is the purpose of our program."

"Remind your students to come to the Christmas parade. We want the kids to enjoy it, too."

"I will."

"Why, I remember the Christmas little Anna Imhoff stood so straight and tall and recited her poem with such a big grin on her face at your school. That was the year they found John Doe beaten half to death on the Imhoff farm. Course, he was really Jonathan Dresher, but he didn't know his own name for weeks. Ain't it strange the ways the Lord finds to test us?" He stopped with her last item in his hand and stared into space.

"It is, indeed." She really needed to be going. She had a long walk home before dark.

"Anna sure took a shine to Jonathan. Happy thing, him

marrying her sister, Karen. Yup, that was a mighty special Christmas."

"*Ja,* it was." Joann winked at Leah. Mr. McGregor loved to recount his stories regardless of the number of times his customers had heard them.

The outside door opened, and Leah saw an *Englisch* fellow come in. There was something vaguely familiar about him. He glanced her way.

Her breath caught in her throat. It couldn't be Caleb Mast, could it?

He turned down the collar of his coat and headed to the back of the store without any hint that he recognized her.

"Leah, is something wrong?" Joann gave her a funny look.

"Did you see the man who just walked in?"

"*Nee.*" Joann looked toward the back of the store.

"I think it was Caleb Mast." Leah was almost sure of it.

"Really? I wonder what he's doing in Hope Springs after all this time. How long has it been?"

Leah knew exactly how long he had been gone. Nine years ago this month she was to have married his brother, Wayne. Then Caleb ruined everything.

Mr. McGregor rang up the rest of Leah's order. "How did that poem go again? 'On a night so bitter and dark, in a land far, far away, a tiny child was born and laid in a manger of hay.' Is that how it went?"

Her gaze followed Caleb. He was searching for something in the cookie aisle. Why was he back? Had he come to regret his break with his family and his faith?

He glanced her way. She realized she was staring and quickly looked down. What would she do if he spoke to her?

Nothing. Ignore him. There wasn't anything to say. The past couldn't be changed. Maybe he hadn't recognized her.

"How did it go again?" Mr. McGregor asked.

She forced her attention back to the grocer. "What?"

"The Christmas poem Anna recited. How did it go?"

"I'm afraid I don't remember offhand. I have a copy at school. I'll send it to you." She handed over her money, suddenly eager to leave the store. She grabbed her bag of groceries and rushed out the door.

Joann followed her. "Are you all right?"

In the cold air outside, Leah paused to draw a deep breath and recover from her shock. Seeing Caleb made her realize she'd been lying to herself for years.

She hadn't forgiven him. It was against everything her faith stood for.

When her racing heart slowed, she adjusted her dark bonnet over her ears. "I'm fine. Are you coming to help us bake cookies next Wednesday? Sarah and Rebecca have already said they'll be there."

"Of course. What could be more fun than a baking frolic with my friends?"

"Eating our fill, then taking the rest to the cookie exchange on Friday afternoon and getting wonderful new varieties to try in return."

Joann grinned. "My mouth is watering just thinking about it. I'll see you then." She waved as she crossed the street. The printing office was only a few blocks away.

Leah pulled on her mittens. She had a long walk ahead of her. God had allowed winter to take hold of the land. He'd sent a dusting of snow that morning, the first of the season.

She glanced at the grocery store door. Did Caleb's family know he was coming? No one had mentioned it to her. She shivered in the cold.

She shouldn't be standing around thinking about Caleb and the harm he'd caused. She had better things to do. There was a Christmas pageant to finish planning and papers to grade, as well as chores to be done. Whatever had brought Caleb to Hope Springs, it had nothing to do with her.

At least his return would give his mother comfort. Mag-

gie Mast would know her son was alive and well. The only contact Caleb had maintained with his family was an annual Christmas card with a brief note. A card mailed without a return address, although for the past few years the postmark had come from Houston, Texas. Leah knew Maggie cherished every one and kept them in a shoe box beside her bed.

"Mama! Daddy!" The shrill cries of a child startled Leah.

A girl in a pink sweater and stocking feet ran past along the sidewalk. She paused for a moment, turned in frantic circles, crying and calling, and then started running again. At first glance, Leah thought she might have Down syndrome. Clearly, she was distraught.

Looking around, Leah realized there was no one else about. The child paused at the corner, then ran out of sight up the block. Had she found who she was looking for? A second later, Leah heard her calling again. Apparently not.

She couldn't leave a child alone and in distress. She put her bag of groceries on a nearby bench and went after the frightened girl. She caught up with her and took hold of her arm. "There, there, little one, what's the matter?"

"Mama's gone, and Nana's gone, and Daddy is gone, too."

Leah knelt and used her gloves to wipe the tears from her face. She did have Down syndrome. Leah was familiar with such special children. In her years as a teacher, she'd dealt with two *kinder* with the same syndrome. She knew the first thing she needed was to get the child calm enough to answer a few questions. "I'll help you find them. There's no need to cry."

The child threw her arms around Leah's neck and hung on for dear life. Leah rose with the girl in her arms. She looked up and down the street. Where were the parents? She rocked the child gently from side to side to soothe her.

"Calm down, sweetheart. It will be okay. We'll find your folks in a minute. My name is Leah Belier. What's your name?"

"Joy Lynn Perry." A muffled sniff followed the tiny voice.

"I'm very pleased to meet you, Joy Perry. Do you live around here?" Leah started walking in the direction the child had been running.

"I live at one…two…one…seven Hudson Place."

There was no such address in the small village of Hope Springs. "That's very good, Joy. I'm going to guess that you came to town in a car, right?"

"No."

"Then you must have come on the bus. Did you ride the bus to Hope Springs?"

"No."

"Don't tell me you came in a buggy."

"Okay, I won't." Joy lifted her face from Leah's neck. "Can you find my daddy?"

Leah turned around slowly searching the quiet street. "I'd love to find him. Are you staying with someone in town? Are you staying at the inn?"

"No. How come you wear such a funny hat?"

"Is my bonnet funny?" Leah asked with a grin.

Joy nodded solemnly.

If she wasn't familiar with Amish dress, she wasn't staying with any of the Amish families in the area. That narrowed the number of possibilities. "If you didn't come to Hope Springs in a buggy, or a car, or a bus, how did you get here?"

"In daddy's truck."

"Ah, a truck. How silly of me. Can you show me where the truck is parked?"

Joy looked around. "No. It's lost."

Suddenly, Leah heard a man franticly shouting for Joy. "That must be your daddy. Let's go see him."

She began walking back the way she had come. She rounded the corner of the building just as Joy's daddy came running toward her. Leah said, "I have her. She's okay."

In the next instant, she was struck speechless as Caleb Mast pulled the child from her arms and held her close, his ragged gasps rising as white puffs in the cold air.

Looking straight at her, he said, "Thank you, Leah."

He had recognized her, after all. Now what did she do?

Chapter Two

Leah stood rooted to the spot. Caleb had a child. That meant he had a wife, too. He had found happiness and love in the outside world after turning her life upside down. It was so unfair. She couldn't stop the bitterness that welled up inside.

Caleb's mother never mentioned he had married or that he had children. Maybe he hadn't told her. Some outsiders were ashamed of a child who wasn't normal. Had he become one of those?

Leah quickly pulled herself together. Caleb's *Englisch* life was no concern of hers. "She's fine, only a little frightened."

Caleb set his daughter on the ground and took her by the shoulders. "What were you doing? Why did you run off?" he demanded.

"I got scared. I wanna go home." She pushed away from him and covered her ears with her hands.

"Don't do that! I'm not going to hit you."

"I'm not bad. I'm not bad." She flew back to Leah and wrapped her arms around her legs.

He pressed his fingers to his temples and exhaled sharply. "I give up. I don't know what to do with you."

Leah laid a protective hand on Joy's head. "Patience and

kindness are the keys to raising a special child. All children are gifts from God, but we believe a child such as Joy is one of His most cherished gifts."

Caleb's hands dropped to his sides. He looked…defeated. "I know what the Amish believe. That's why I'm here. The only reason I'm here."

She didn't understand. He tipped his head slightly. A mocking smile lifted one corner of his mouth. "The prodigal son has returned. You don't look happy to see me."

She wasn't. She didn't care if he knew it. He had changed a great deal in the past nine years. The wild, handsome Amish boy she had known had matured into a tall, rugged-looking man with a muscular frame and deeply tanned skin. He wore his dark hair cut short in the *Englisch* way, not in the bowl-cut style the men of her community wore. She didn't remember the small scar that cut through his right eyebrow. How had that happened? It was a faded white line now, not like the jagged red scar that still marred her sister Rhonda's face.

An accident, caused by Caleb's recklessness during their teenage years, had cruelly marked her beautiful sister, but it was his later actions that had truly scarred her.

Leah realized he was studying her, too. Watching her with hard, piercing gray eyes that gave away little of what he was thinking. A shiver of awareness raced through her and brought a rush of heat to her face.

His mocking smile widened. "It's good to see you, Leah. Did you marry my brother, or did you come to your senses in time?"

She stiffened. The hurt was old, but it had never healed. "Your brother married Rhonda."

"Wayne married your sister? Wow, I didn't see that coming. Funny how things turn out, isn't it?"

"Funny? It is far from funny." She kept the rest of her angry reply bottled inside only because of the child. How

dare he mock that terrible time? He'd left her sister unwed and pregnant when he ran off to start a new life among the *Englisch*.

"Bad choice of words. I'm sorry."

"Your brother is a man of honor," she said tartly.

He tensed. "And I'm not, is that what you're saying? Oh, if only you knew the truth about my brother and his honor."

"Your deeds speak so loudly that I can't hear what you're saying."

"An Amish proverb for every occasion. I see your quick wit hasn't changed. I do remember that about you."

"And I have not forgotten the way you denied your own child. The way you called my sister a liar to her face. You shamed us all."

Caleb had held only a faint hope that Rhonda Belier would have admitted the truth sometime during the past nine years. Clearly she hadn't. He wasn't the father of her child. They had dated, but they had never been intimate. He had no idea who the father might be.

That Wayne had fallen on the sword of family honor and married her came as a shock. Had his guilt driven him to it? Had Wayne owned up to his past sins, or was he still using Caleb as a handy scapegoat? From Leah's reaction, Caleb figured he himself still bore all the blame. He struggled to suppress those unpleasant memories. Nothing hurt as much as knowing his family and friends had turned their collective backs on him. No one had believed his side of the story. Not his parents, not even his brother, and that hurt most of all.

Caleb had always been the wild one, the one in trouble, the one eager to rebel against the constraints of their closed community. He had badgered and baited his brother into going to a party where he knew there would be drinking that night. He'd thought Wayne deserved one night of fun

before he settled down to marry. Caleb had owned a forbidden car. He'd goaded his brother into driving it. Hours later, when Caleb had learned that Wayne had crashed into Rhonda's buggy, he had been sick with remorse.

Wayne had managed to make his way home, terrified, almost incoherent with fear and shame. He thought he had killed Rhonda. When Caleb realized that no one knew about the accident, he had quickly gone to the crash site. He'd discovered Rhonda was alive but injured and had summoned help for her. He'd allowed everyone to think he had been the one driving. He had stoically endured the shame heaped on him by his family and the community. He knew he deserved it even if he hadn't been behind the wheel. He had done it to shield his big brother, the one who could do no wrong in their father's eyes.

Months later, when Caleb begged Wayne to believe he hadn't fathered Rhonda's child, Wayne refused to accept Caleb's word. It had been the final blow in their relationship.

Caleb shrugged off his resentment. He'd made a choice to come back. Now he had to face the consequences of that decision. Hopefully he wasn't going to be here long. Leah's brown eyes fairly snapped with anger. He could see she wanted to say a lot more. He figured the only reason she wasn't reading him the riot act was because Joy was listening.

He remembered Leah as a skinny girl with wide brown eyes and a tendency to speak her mind. She'd been someone who found the world and everyone in it of interest. She'd seemed an odd pick for his self-righteous brother back then. He'd found it hard to imagine her in love with Wayne.

She certainly wasn't a skinny kid anymore. Even under her long coat, he could tell she had filled out in all the right places. A black bonnet covered all but the front of her honey-blond hair. Like all Amish women, she wore it

parted in the center and coiled into a bun at the back of her head. Amish women never cut their hair.

Her plump cheeks were pink with cold or perhaps her anger. He wasn't sure which. Had she married? The Amish didn't believe in jewelry of any kind, not even wedding bands, so he had no way of knowing. What did it matter anyway?

"I don't know why your sister lied about me. I'm sure she thought she had a good reason." A lie told for any reason only led to more lies and heartache. He had learned that bitter lesson well.

He turned his attention to his daughter. "Come on, Joy, we should get going. You didn't put your coat or your shoes on. You're going to freeze out here." He reached to pick her up.

She jerked away and hid behind Leah's skirt. "I don't wanna go with you. I wanna go to Nana's house. I don't like you anymore."

Leah's eyes narrowed. A frown creased her brow. He shook his head. Trust Joy to make him look like a bad parent. Leah would have no trouble believing her.

Well, he *was* a poor excuse for a parent. If he'd learned anything in the weeks since Valerie's vanishing act, it was that he had no idea how to be a father.

"We've had this talk, honey. You can't go back to Dallas. Nana isn't there anymore. She's gone to heaven." He tried to reason with Joy although he knew it wouldn't do any good when she got in one of her moods.

"Go away. I want *Mama* to come get me."

He threw up his hands. "So do I, but it looks like that's not going to happen."

He pressed his lips shut. It wasn't Joy's fault Valerie had dumped her like an unwanted dog. He understood how difficult all the changes must be for her, but what choice did they have? "It's not far to your new grandma's house. You

want to meet her, don't you?" he asked calmly. He tried again to catch hold of her.

"No!" She pulled away from him and looked up at Leah. "I wanna go home with you."

He shoved his hands in his coat pockets. "Fine! Guess I get to eat the animal crackers that are in the truck. I'm going to bite the heads off all the elephants."

Joy glared at him but didn't rise to his bait. The mulish expression on her face did not bode well. He sighed. No matter what he did, no matter how hard he tried, he couldn't make a connection with her. She hated him.

"Please, Joy. We need to get going. Say thank-you to Leah and come on."

"No, no, no!" She dropped down on the sidewalk, screaming and kicking her legs.

Now his face flushed with embarrassment as people coming out of the store stopped to stare. He glanced at Leah. What was she thinking? Perhaps it was best that he didn't know. He shook his head. "I'm sorry."

Her gaze softened slightly. "I've seen a temper tantrum or two in my time."

"Any suggestions on how to deal with them?" He was willing to take any help he could get. He kept a close eye on Joy so she didn't hurt herself.

"I'm sure as her father you know what's best for her."

He ran a hand over his hair. "I've been her father for a total of six weeks and three days. Believe me, I have no idea what's best for her. Pick her up. Don't pick her up. Let her cry it out, put her in time-out. Ignore her. Distract her. Reason with her. I've had all kinds of advice from the two nannies who both quit within a week, from the principal of an expensive private school that wouldn't take her after the first day, and from her step-grandfather, who said to throw water in her face, it worked for him."

"Did you?"

He glanced at Leah and saw her regarding him intently. She hadn't scurried away and left him to deal with the situation alone. His respect for her jumped considerably. Joy continued to kick and scream.

"No. I almost threw water in *his* face, but I left before I did something I knew I would regret."

"Very wise. Very Amish. Where's your truck?"

"On the other side of the store." He tipped his head in the general direction. He was ex-Amish, not Amish.

Leah bent down and lifted Joy. His daughter wasn't a lightweight, but Leah had no trouble carrying her. She held the screaming child close and started walking. "We're going to the truck now, Joy. It will be warmer there. As soon as you calm down, we will talk about what's upsetting you."

Caleb followed, happy for once to have someone else take charge. When they reached the truck, he stepped ahead to open the passenger-side door. To his surprise, Leah didn't deposit Joy inside. Instead, she climbed in and held Joy on her lap.

He walked around to the driver's side and rescued his scattered groceries from the sidewalk where he'd dropped them when he discovered Joy was missing. Opening his door, he set them behind the driver's seat on the king cab's rear bench seat. He climbed in behind the wheel, at a lost as to what to do next.

He wanted to take Joy from Leah, but he was afraid it would make things worse. He started the engine. After a few minutes, warm air filled the cab. He noticed the soothing way Leah rocked Joy and consoled her. Joy's sobs were growing less dire.

He gripped the steering wheel. His parental shortcomings were laid bare once more. Joy would take comfort from a stranger before she took it from him. At least Leah seemed to know how to handle his daughter. He glanced her way. "Thanks for your help. Again."

"I do it for the child," she said primly.

He got the message. "Not for the father who strayed from the Amish fold."

She looked directly at him. "*Nee,* not for you."

Leah continued to hold and rock Joy until the child calmed down. Spent by her outburst, she rested in Leah's arms with only occasional hiccupping sobs to break the awkward silence. Leah brushed Joy's fine, soft hair away from her face and glanced at Caleb. Did he know how blessed he was to have this child?

She was forever comforting, caring for and teaching children who belonged to others. Her profession was a labor of love, a sacred duty, but it wasn't like having children of her own. The unfairness of it cut deep. She longed to hold her own babe. She didn't understand why God had chosen this path for her. She could only travel it as best she could and trust in His mercy.

After a few minutes, Joy sat up. She looked at her father. "Can I have an elephant now?"

Caleb reached behind the seat and brought out a red-and-yellow box made to look like a circus wagon, with colorful animals printed on the sides. He handed it to her. There were several similar boxes on the floor of the truck.

He must have noticed Leah's gaze. "Sometimes they keep her from having a meltdown like the one you just witnessed. I stopped to stock up before heading out to the farm. She was sound asleep when I went in the store. I couldn't have been gone more than five minutes."

Leah didn't want to feel sorry for him, but she couldn't help it. It was easy to see that he didn't know how to handle his newly acquired daughter. What was the story behind his cryptic comment about only being a father for six weeks? Had he adopted a special-needs child? Curiosity,

often her downfall, prompted her to remain in the truck and learn more about Caleb and Joy.

Joy opened the box and picked out two elephant-shaped cookies. She looked at Leah. "Do you want one?"

Leah held out a hand. "May I have a lion?"

"Okay, sure." Joy extracted two of them, laid the pair in Leah's palm and gave her an endearing grin.

Children with Down syndrome were normally happy, gregarious individuals. Leah loved that about them. "What shall we give your daddy?"

"A bear," Joy said quickly.

Leah glanced at him from the corner of her eye. His daughter's remark caused a reluctant grin to tug at one side of his mouth. "Is that your way of telling me I'm as grumpy as an old bear?"

Leah leaned over to see Joy's face. "Is your daddy grumpy?"

"Sometimes." Cookie crumbs sprayed from her lips. She handed him three bears.

"I get grumpy sometimes, too," Leah admitted. "So do you. What made you so upset a little while ago?"

The child bowed her head. "I don't know."

"I think you do. Your daddy can't fix things for you if he doesn't know what's wrong."

"He wants me to go away."

"That's not true," Caleb said quickly.

"I wanna go home and be with Nana. I want Mama to come get me and take me home. She'll never find me here." She laid her head on Leah's shoulder and closed her eyes.

Leah glanced to Caleb for an explanation. He shook his head slightly. Whatever the story was, he didn't want to recount it in front of the child. Another awkward minute of silence passed.

Joy sat up and cupped Leah's face with her hands. "I'm sorry I was bad."

Leah's heart turned over. What a sweet child. "You are forgiven. You will like your *grossmammi* when you meet her, and she will love you."

Joy tipped her head to the side. "What's that?"

"*Grossmammi?* It's the Amish word for grandmother."

"Oh. What's an Amish?"

Leah chuckled. "I am Amish. We are a Plain People who believe in remaining separate from worldly things and living a simple life so that we may live close to God and each other."

"You're not plain. You're pretty."

"So are you." Leah gave her a quick hug. "But I need to be going. It's getting late. I have a long walk home."

"Don't go!" Joy threw her arms around Leah's neck and held on tight.

"Joy, stop that. She has to go." Caleb tried to pull her arms loose.

"No," she sobbed, and held on tighter.

"Stop. You're hurting me. Let go and we will talk about it," Leah said firmly.

Joy slowly released her grip. "I'm not bad."

Leah waited for Caleb to say something, but he seemed at a loss for words. She took Joy's hands and met her gaze. "No one said you are bad. However, your behavior just now was not very nice."

"I want you to be my friend. I don't want you to go away."

"I am your friend, but I have to go home. You have to go meet your grandparents."

Caleb spoke at last. "Let me give you a lift home. It's the least I can do after all your help."

Leah could see Joy was on the verge of another breakdown. She hated giving in. It wouldn't teach Joy self-control if she got her way with her tantrums. Still, Leah didn't want to be the cause of another episode. She hadn't forgiven

Caleb for the way he had treated her sister, but ignoring someone in distress, especially a child, wasn't something she could do. Allowing Joy a chance to calm down might make their parting easier. "That's kind of you to offer, Caleb. *Danki.*"

"Great." His relief was almost comical.

Leah put her hand on the door handle. "I left a bag of groceries on the bench in front of the store. Could you get it for me, Joy?"

"Okay. You won't go away before I get back, will you?"

"I will wait right here."

"Put your shoes and coat on first," Caleb said.

Joy climbed in the backseat, pulled her sneakers and jacket on, then climbed over Leah to get out.

Caleb relaxed as he watched his daughter run to pick up the grocery bag. "You're very good with kids, Leah. How many do you have?"

"An entire school full."

He scowled for a second and then smiled. A warm and genuine smile that smoothed the lines of worry from his brow. He was handsome in a rugged way that many women would find attractive. She refused to be one of them. A kind heart was more important than a handsome face.

"I assume that means you're a teacher?"

"*Ja,* at Walnut Valley School."

"The same one we attended as kids? That's got to feel strange."

"Not so much. Do you mind if I ask what happened to Joy's mother?"

His scowl reappeared. "To make a long story short, Valerie and I were together for a year after I left here. One day, I came home and found a note telling me she was leaving. It wasn't until the next day I found out she had cleaned out our bank account and left me with a pile of debts that took me three years to pay off."

His life hadn't been easy out among the *Englisch*. Leah found small comfort in the thought. Her life hadn't been easy, either.

"I didn't hear from her again until she turned up at my door in the middle of the night a month and a half ago. She had Joy with her. She told me I was Joy's father. She went out to smoke a cigarette and never came back."

He had been abandoned the same way he had abandoned her pregnant sister. The irony wasn't lost on Leah, but she saved her pity for Joy.

She looked out the window to see what was keeping her. A horse and buggy had pulled up in front of the store. Joy stood transfixed by the sight. A woman and a young girl got out. Leah recognized Karen Dresher and her young sister, Anna Imhoff. Anna was eleven and one of Leah's brightest students.

Caleb continued speaking. "My attorney helped me track down Valerie's stepfather. I learned Joy's grandmother raised her until her death a few months ago. Valerie came and went over the years. She took Joy with her a few times but always brought her back. The kid's had a rough life."

"No wonder she was terrified when she woke and you were gone. She needs stability, a sense of home and security. You are right to return to your family. Among us you will both find acceptance and peace." Leah meant her words, although she knew it would be difficult for everyone involved, particularly her sister, to accept Caleb back into the family.

Outside, Karen and Anna were talking to Joy. Anna was encouraging her to pet the horse's nose. Leah smiled and waved to them. Karen waved in return.

"I'm hoping Joy will find acceptance here, but the Amish life isn't for me," Caleb said.

Leah whipped around to stare at him in shock. "After

all your child has been through you mean to abandon her, too? How can you be so heartless?"

To think she had spared one ounce of pity for him. She fumbled for the door handle, determined to leave before she said more. He leaned across the seat and grabbed her arm to stop her.

Chapter Three

"It isn't like that. I'm not dumping her off the way her mother did."

Caleb needed all the help he could get. He couldn't let Leah leave thinking less of him than she already did. If that was possible.

As a teacher, Leah would be an important part of Joy's life in the Amish community, second only to his parents if they agreed to raise her. He wanted Leah on his side. On Joy's side.

Leah stopped trying to open the door and glared at him. "What is it like?"

He let go of her arm. "I put a great-paying job on hold when Joy arrived in my life. I've tried to give her what she needs, but my one-bedroom condo isn't exactly set up for family living. I've come back where I know I'm not welcome because I want Joy to have a home. A place she will always belong. A place where she will be loved and valued.

"Yes, I'll be leaving, but not until I'm certain she can be happy here and that this is the best thing for her. If that takes two months or twelve months, I'll stay that long. Honestly, I doubt she'll even miss me."

"How can she have such happiness without her father or her mother?"

"I'm her father in name only. She barely knows me. Her mother… I can't even talk about Valerie without getting angry."

He drew a deep breath to calm down. After a few seconds, he said, "I know Val had it rough. Joy can go from sweet to those horrible tantrums in five seconds flat. I didn't know kids with Down could be that way. I thought they were always happy and loving."

Having a special-needs child had been a rude awakening for Caleb. He'd had no idea what to expect. As he struggled to adjust, he found himself wanting to shout at the people who looked away when they saw Joy was different, as if seeing her somehow disturbed them.

Her step-grandfather had talked about her as if she wasn't in the room with him, calling her stupid and a pain. Even in the few weeks she had lived with Caleb, a dozen people told him how sorry they were that he had a retarded child. Joy deserved better. He didn't know how else he could give her a chance to be accepted for who she was.

Leah didn't say anything so he went on. "Joy has learned not to trust people. Especially men. Her step-grandfather is a prime example. My attorney uncovered reports of abuse in the home. Her life when she was with her mother wasn't any better. Val has a drug problem. I believe she tried to be good to Joy, but she couldn't even take care of herself, let alone a kid."

"I'm sorry Joy has known such unhappiness."

"Do you see why I know she'll be better off here? You'll be her teacher. You'll see her nearly every day. With your help, Joy can learn to trust again. She'll be cared for and loved by the Amish community her whole life. She'll never be made to feel inferior. I want her to have that."

He'd tried to give Joy that kind of life in Houston, but he had failed miserably. He'd thought leaving the Amish was hard. It was nothing compared to the changes he had

to make in his life when Valerie dropped Joy in his lap without so much as a toothbrush. Could he make Leah understand that?

"Joy can be a charming child, but she doesn't adapt to change well. Her way of coping is to fall down and have a screaming fit or simply run away, which she did numerous times in the first four weeks with me. She wanted to go find her mother. She had it in her little brain that her mother would come get her if she went back to Nana's house.

"The police officers in my part of town knew us on a first-name basis. I lived in a constant state of fear. I couldn't take my eyes off her. The last time, when Joy was found walking along the middle of a freeway, I reached my breaking point. Something had to give."

Leah looked down and smoothed the front of her coat. "If you think so highly of our community, why haven't you returned to us before now?"

He didn't care to explain the complex reasons why he'd left and why he'd stayed away. "This isn't about me. It's about Joy. Do you honestly believe she is better off with me? I don't think so. You believe she'll be better off as part of the Amish community, too. Will you help her?"

Caleb studied Leah's face as she considered his question. If only he knew what she was thinking. She looked out the window toward his daughter. Joy was grinning from ear to ear as she patted the horse. She took a step back and clapped her chubby hands together, then reached up to touch him again.

"The school board will have to approve her transfer to our school," Leah said at last.

He hadn't considered that. "Do you think it will be a problem?"

"Perhaps. She is *Englisch,* after all. They may feel she should attend the *Englisch* school in town. Your parents

may need to plead her case and state their desire to raise her in the Amish way. Will they do that?"

"All I can do is ask."

His mother would welcome Joy with open arms. He wasn't so sure about his father. He had to believe they would agree with his decision to bring her here. If not, he didn't know what he would do. Joy needed more than he could give her.

"I should tell you that Wayne is on the school board."

"I see." Would his brother block his efforts?

"No matter where she continues her education, you'll need her records from her last school. Do you have them?"

"She was homeschooled by her grandmother."

"Can you get copies of her curriculum and any test scores? Each state has different requirements. I'm not familiar with what Texas requires."

"I'll have my attorney get what he can and send it to me." Caleb had already paid the firm a big chunk of his savings to gain temporary custody of Joy. Whatever it took, he was willing to do. His one overriding fear was that Valerie could get Joy back and all of this would have been for nothing.

Leah stared at him for a long moment. "What happens when Joy's mother returns for her and wants to take her away?"

He shifted his gaze to his hands on the steering wheel. It was a question he couldn't answer. He wanted Joy to know security and happiness. His attorney was working to sever Valerie's parental rights on the basis of abandonment, but Caleb wasn't sure what would happen if she returned to fight for custody.

"I left a letter for Valerie with her stepfather and one with my attorney if she should come looking for us. I let her know I was taking Joy to my folks. She knows they're Amish. I'm hoping she'll realize that Joy is better off with them and stay out of her life."

"Shouldn't you pray that she sees the error of her ways and wants to reunite with her daughter?"

"You can pray for that if you want. I won't waste my time. God doesn't listen to me." Caleb had stopped praying a long time ago.

Sadness filled Leah's eyes. "God hears everyone's prayers. Perhaps you are the one who has stopped listening for His answer."

He tipped his head to the side and tried for a lighter tone. "Maybe you should pray for me, then."

Her chin came up a notch at his challenge. "I will, Caleb Mast. I will do just that."

Joy finished petting the horse, picked up the grocery bag and came running toward the truck. He got out and held open the door as she raced around the hood.

"Did you see me? I touched a horse, a real horse. Not a pretend one. His name is Benny. He belongs to Anna. I want a horse."

He smiled at her excitement. Taking the bag of groceries from her, he handed them to Leah and then lifted his daughter into the truck. "You'll meet lots of horses at your grandpa and grandma's farm. Cows, too, and chickens and ducks, but no elephants."

"Do they have a dog?"

Caleb glanced at Leah. "Do they?"

"They don't have a dog, but I do. Her name is Trixie, and she is going to have puppies soon. I've been trying to think of some names for them. Have you got any suggestions?"

Caleb breathed an inward sigh of relief. Leah seemed to be on board with his plan. While she might not like helping him, he had to trust that she would do what was best for Joy.

He drove out of town with a renewed sense of hope. This might actually work. If Joy was happy and safe, he couldn't ask for more.

"If your dog has a girl puppy, you can call it Princess," Joy said from the backseat.

Caleb smothered a grin and waited for Leah's reply. She tilted her head slightly. "I think Princess is much too fancy a name for an Amish dog. She will be a working dog."

"What kind of work can a dog do?" Joy asked.

"My puppies will grow up to herd sheep and cattle, just like their mother and father do."

Caleb glanced at Leah. "Are they border collies?"

"English shepherds."

The breed wasn't well-known outside farming communities. Similar to the border collie in size and coat texture, they were often sable and white or tricolor. Unlike many herding dogs, English shepherds were used to guard as well as herd cattle, sheep, goats, pigs and even fowl. They made excellent farm dogs.

"Pete would be a good name," Caleb suggested.

"Not for a girl dog, Daddy," Joy said in disgust.

"Right. Not for a girl dog," he conceded.

Leah half turned in the seat to speak to Joy. "Can you think of another name?"

Joy was thinking, so Caleb ventured a second suggestion. "Matilda."

"No." Joy shook her head. "I don't like that name."

"Okay, how about Tilly? It rhymes with *silly*," Leah said.

He glanced at his daughter's face in the rearview mirror. She grinned at Leah. "No, not Silly Tilly. I like Pickles."

"*Ja,* I like pickles, too. Dill pickles, sweet pickles, even bread-and-butter pickles. Do you like pickles, Caleb?"

"I do. I like pickles on sandwiches and on hamburgers. I like to eat the little crispy ones right out of the jar."

Joy shook her head. "Not pickles to eat. Pickles for a name. I want to call the puppy Pickles."

"*Ach,* I see." Leah nodded solemnly. "Pickles is an ex-

cellent name. If my Trixie has a girl puppy, her name will be Pickles."

They'd gone only half a mile down the highway when they came upon a buggy traveling in the same direction. Caleb slowed to a crawl, unable to pass on the hilly road.

"Does your family know you're coming?" Leah asked.

"I wrote. I wasn't sure when to tell them to expect us." He hadn't mailed the letter until the day they left. Up until the moment he dropped the letter in the mailbox, he'd hoped he could find a way to manage his life with Joy in Texas. Admitting that he couldn't was a bitter pill to swallow. He simply didn't know where else to turn.

Leah lapsed into silence until he had the chance to pass the buggy. As they went by, she sat back and muttered, "Oh, no."

"What?" He looked in his rearview mirror but didn't see anything amiss.

"That was Esther Zook."

"The bishop's wife?"

"The same."

"Has she changed any in the past decade?"

"*Nee,* she has not."

"So gossip about you riding with an *Englisch* fellow will be spreading before the sun sets tomorrow. Good to know some things never change. Will it be better or worse for you when she learns it was me?"

"You were not baptized. No one must shun you."

"Some people will think I should be."

"Not everyone has a forgiving nature, in spite of what we are taught."

He glanced at her. "Do you?"

"Have a forgiving nature? I thought so, but I find it is something I must work on."

It wasn't the answer he wanted. For some reason, he wanted to know that she had forgiven him for leaving the

Amish, for straying so far from the path laid out from his birth. It was a foolish thought. He was grateful she was willing to consider teaching Joy. That was enough.

"I live in the same house. It's past the next hill on the right-hand side of the road, a short mile after the school."

"You still live with your folks?"

"*Nee,* they are gone now."

"I'm sorry." He slowed as he topped the rise. The school building and schoolyard were just as he remembered them. He would have to tell Joy to look for his name carved under one of the desks. The lane to Leah's home came all too quickly. He turned in and hoped Joy would say goodbye without making a fuss.

Her face took on the mulish pout he dreaded, once Leah opened the door to get out.

She held out her hand to Joy. "It was wonderful meeting you. I look forward to seeing you at school."

"At school?" Joy gave her a puzzled look.

"Your father wants to enroll you in my school. If it works out, I'll be your new teacher. Wouldn't that great?"

Joy folded her arms over her chest and stared at the floor of the truck. "I don't like school. Other kids make fun of me."

"My students won't do that. Besides, even if you don't come to my school, I'm sure your father will bring you over to see the puppies when they arrive."

Joy looked at Caleb. "Will you?"

"Sure, kiddo."

Joy clapped her hands and rewarded him with a beaming smile that crinkled her eyes closed. He smiled in return. It was amazing how fast he was growing to love her. That was one more reason to get her settled quickly. Another painful upheaval wouldn't do either of them any good.

He glanced at Leah. She was smiling at Joy, too. As their eyes met, his heart gave a funny kick. She really was

a pretty woman. He liked the way her eyes sparkled when she smiled.

The last thing he expected to find in Hope Springs was an Amish woman who caught his fancy.

If only things had been different.

And that was the story of his life.

Leah looked away first. "Goodbye, Joy. Be sure and tell your *grossmammi* I said hello."

"I will." Joy waved.

Leah waved, too, and closed the door.

Caleb sat and watched until she entered the house. After a few minutes, the soft glow of lantern light lit the windows. He couldn't put it off any longer. It was time to go home. He shifted the truck in Reverse and began to back up.

"Daddy, stop!"

He hit the brakes. "What?"

"Leah wants you."

He looked toward the house. She stood on the porch motioning to him. He put the truck in Park. Was something wrong? He looked around the cab. He didn't see anything she might have left behind.

"Stay here, Joy." He opened his door.

"But I want to come in."

"We're not staying. I'm just going to see what Leah wants." He stepped out of the truck. The light layer of powdery fresh snow muffled his footsteps as he crossed the yard to her porch.

Leah's eyes were bright with excitement. As he neared, that excitement faded. She bit her lower lip and clasped her hands together nervously. When she didn't speak, he asked, "Is something wrong?"

"*Nee.* It's only that Trixie has had her puppies. I thought perhaps Joy would like to see them."

Bemused by her unexpected offer, he hitched a thumb toward his truck. "I'm sure she will. I'll go get her."

He was happy to put off going home for a bit longer. The real upside was spending more time in Leah's company.

What was she thinking?

Leah couldn't believe she had just invited Caleb Mast into her home. She had been so excited to find the puppies had arrived that she had simply stepped out and beckoned Joy to come see them, not thinking that Caleb would come, too. She could hardly ask him to wait outside while she took his child in. She prayed her sister wouldn't find out.

Leah watched as Caleb lifted Joy out of the truck. He spoke to her quietly and then held her hand as they approached the house. Leah stood aside and let them enter.

She had placed the whelping box in the kitchen, near the stove for warmth. Trixie lay on an old quilt in a corner of the box with three tiny black, brown and white pups nestled against her belly. She pricked up her ears and gave the newcomers a guarded look.

Trixie was a medium-size dog with long black fur and a white blaze that went down her face and chest. Over her eyes and upright ears, she had brown points, which gave her an inquisitive look. Two of the puppies were marked like their mother. A third was as pale brown as winter grass, with a white blaze and chest and four white feet.

Leah spoke quietly to reassure her. "It's okay. They want to admire your babies."

Joy knelt beside the box with Caleb at her side. "They are super awesome. Can I touch them, Daddy?" Her voice squeaked with excitement.

He brushed a lock of hair away from her eyes. "You have to ask to Leah. Remember, I said we have to talk very quietly so we don't disturb them."

She nodded and looked up at Leah. "Can I touch them?" she whispered.

"I think Trixie will allow that." She reached into the box

and lifted a tiny ball of fur. The puppy mewed at having its sleep cut short. Trixie rose to her feet and stood close as Leah handed the pup to Joy, showing her how to hold it properly.

Joy raised the puppy to her face. "Oh, it's so soft. It this Pickles?"

"Let me see." Caleb took the puppy from her and checked the gender. "Yup, this is Pickles." He handed her back to his daughter.

Joy pressed her close. "I love you, Pickles."

The puppy started crying, making Trixie whine with concern. Leah said, "We should put Pickles back with her mother now. She needs lots of rest so she can grow up to be a wonderful helper on someone's farm."

Joy handed her back to Leah. Trixie nosed her pup and licked her as Leah replaced her with her littermates. Joy looked at Leah. "Pickles's mommy will take good care of her. She won't run away and leave her to be scared."

Leah exchanged a poignant look with Caleb. They were both thinking the same thing. Joy was referring to her own mother's actions. Caleb put an arm around her. "No, Trixie is going to take good care of all her puppies."

Joy pushed his arm away and looked around the kitchen. "Where is their daddy?"

Leah knelt beside her. "His name is Duncan. He lives on a sheep farm not far from here with his master."

Joy frowned. "Does he ever come to visit his kids?"

Leah smothered a smile. "They were only born today. I'm sure he'll be by when he hears the news."

"He better come. He shouldn't be a deadbeat dad. My friends Jenny and Kala have deadbeat dads."

Puzzled, Leah said, "What does that mean?"

Caleb rose to his feet. His demeanor changed as he squared off, almost as if he expected a fight. "A deadbeat

dad is a man who doesn't take responsibility for his children, doesn't visit them or help support them."

She rose, too, as the past came rushing in to spoil the moment. "Your *Englisch* world must be a sad place if such a thing is common there."

Caleb took Joy's hand. "It can be sad. It can be wonderful, too, just like here. Say goodbye to the puppies and thank Leah for letting you see them. We have to get going."

"Thank you. Take good care of Pickles. I like her the best."

Leah spoke before he made it out the door. "The school board is meeting next Thursday evening at Eli Imhoff's home. You are welcome to come and speak with them."

"All right." He didn't say anything else.

Leah closed the door as the pair left, and watched through the kitchen window as they got into Caleb's truck. Rarely had she been so torn about what her course should be.

If she aided his daughter to become Amish, was she helping him avoid responsibilities to a child for a second time?

He genuinely cared about Joy. She saw it in the way he touched his daughter and in the way he spoke to her. He was trying hard to do the right thing.

Why hadn't he given that kind of care and attention to her sister and their unborn child?

Could a man change that much?

With God, anything was possible. If Caleb had changed, why continue to deny he was David's father? He no longer had an obligation to marry her sister or take care of David. Admitting the truth wouldn't change anything except to free his soul from the burden of his lie. It didn't make sense.

Perhaps he was too prideful to admit the truth. That she could believe, yet it was too simple an answer. There had

to be more. Something was holding Caleb apart from the Amish community and from his family. Something painful. What was it?

Chapter Four

Caleb turned his truck onto the narrow dirt lane leading to his childhood home and stopped. It was almost dark. A crimson band of clouds in the west marked the end of the day and a new start to Joy's life.

Up ahead, a large two-story white farmhouse stood nestled into the slope of a hill. It was backed by a thick stand of trees. Their branches were bare now, a mat of dark lines scratching against the bloodred sky. His mother's laundry hung freeze-drying in the winter air from the clothesline at the side of the house. White sheets, blue dresses, blue work shirts, black aprons and dark denim pants. The color palette was the same as it had been throughout his childhood.

He'd thought he was prepared to come back, but he wasn't. A rush of emotions and memories hit him like a truck and then parked on his chest, making it hard to breathe. Scenes from the wonderful years of his youth and the heartbreaking months before he left flickered through his mind like old movie clips.

Working in the fields with his father, driving a team of mules for the first time. Hot summertime days spent shucking corn, followed by a dip in the cool river with his brother. His mother, calling everyone in to eat the most

wonderful meals. His father, bowing his head in prayer. They were good memories.

Then there were the not-so-good memories. The wreck that scarred Rhonda. The bitter arguments with his parents during his *rumspringa,* his teenage years, when he tried to sample all that wasn't Amish. He was introduced to Valerie during that time at a friend's house in Cleveland. She was quite simply the most exciting woman he'd ever met. To remain Amish or to go out into the English world became a real question in his mind for the first time.

Then Rhonda Belier's accusation that he was the father of her unborn babe changed everything. No matter how he denied it, his family expected him to do the right thing and marry her. Nothing he said made any difference until the night he flatly refused to marry her in front of both their families. Leah had been there, but he'd barely noticed her in the room. How did she remember that night? He kept begging Rhonda to admit the truth, but her silence had condemned him. It was the worst night of his life.

What followed was an unofficial shunning by his father. For days, Ike Mast acted as if Caleb wasn't present. He was waiting for a confession that his son couldn't make. Caleb wouldn't take the blame. Not this time. As painful as his father's shunning had been, it was Wayne's refusal to believe Caleb that had finally driven him away.

He shook off the disturbing images from his past and looked around. This stretch of farmland amid the gentle rolling hills of Ohio was, and always would be, home. Too bad it wasn't where he belonged.

What would his life have been like if he had stayed? He couldn't imagine bending far enough to fit into the mold he had been expected to fill.

If he had married Rhonda, Leah would be married to Wayne and not teaching school. She might have children

of her own by now. She would make a good mother. She certainly had a way with Joy.

Why hadn't she married? Was her love for Wayne so strong that she couldn't care for another? He hoped that wasn't the case. Watching the man she loved marry her sister couldn't have been easy. What was their relationship like now? Did Wayne love his wife and the child that wasn't his? What must that be like?

Caleb rubbed a hand over the stubble on his cheeks. His actions had affected far more people than he knew. Leaving had seemed like his only option, but had it been a mistake?

Joy, on the front seat beside him, stretched to see over the dashboard. Was he making another mistake bringing her here? He could turn around now and find a job somewhere, working on an oil rig that wasn't a hundred miles out in the Gulf. He could be home every night. There had to be someplace they could belong and make a go of it.

Even as the thought came to him, he realized Joy hadn't been happy since she had come to him. This was his last hope.

She pointed off to the side. "I see tepees. Lots of them."

The field on the left-hand side of the lane had shocks of cornstalks stacked to provide winter feed for the animals. The long lines of bundles stretched in straight rows across the twenty-acre field. It was hot, itchy work in the summer, piling the stalks together and tying the tops so they would cure properly and not blow over in the wind. He didn't miss that job.

"They aren't tepees, but they do look like them. They're cornstalks."

"They don't look like corn."

"They don't?"

"No, corn is yellow and it comes from a can."

He smiled. She had a lot to learn about living on a farm. He hadn't prayed much in the past nine years, but he si-

lently sent up a plea now. *Please, Lord. Let this be the right decision for her.*

He drove down the lane and stopped in front of the house. A buggy with a black horse in harness stood at the front gate. Did it belong to his folks or did they have company?

For Joy's sake, he didn't want his reunion to occur in front of strangers. He considered driving away, but the front door opened and his mother came out. She stood on the steps, watching him.

He looked at his daughter. There had been so much upheaval in her life. Was he doing the right thing by bringing her here? He couldn't manage on his own. He had tried and failed miserably. He had to believe this was the right thing. "Are you ready to meet your grandparents?"

She shrank back in the seat. "What if they don't like me?"

"They will love you."

"What if they laugh at me or call me stupid?"

He took her chin in his fingers and tilted her face toward him. "I know this is very hard for you. I wish things were different, but they aren't. Do you see that woman standing in the doorway? She is your grandma. I'm one hundred percent certain that she will never laugh at you, never make fun of you. She will love you with her whole heart and soul."

"You promise?"

"I promise. She's waiting to meet you. Are you ready?"

"I guess."

"Then I guess I'm ready, too." That was a lie. Petrified was closer to the truth.

Opening the truck door, he stepped out. His mother came rushing toward him. Behind her, he saw his father looking on from the doorway. Ike Mast did not rush out. He turned away and went back inside. Caleb swallowed the hurt. It was what he had expected.

His mother's steps faltered as she drew near. Her hands were clenched tightly together in front of her. Her eyes searched his face. "Caleb, is it really you?"

He was stunned to see how much she had aged. A black prayer *kapp* covered her gray-streaked hair. She wore a black apron over a blue dress like the ones on the clothesline. She hadn't bothered to put on a coat.

"*Ja, Mamm,* it's me." His throat closed with emotion. He couldn't say another word. None was needed. With a glad cry, she launched herself at him and threw her arms around him.

"*Mein sohn es* home. *Gott* be praised."

He held her for a long moment as he struggled to regain his composure. She was happy to see him now, but he was going to break her heart all over again when he left. He choked back tears and pulled away.

"*Mamm,* I have someone who wants to meet you. This is my daughter, Joy. Did you get my letter about her?"

His mother dabbed her tears away with the corner of her apron. "*Ja,* I did. Welcome to our home, Joy. My name is Maggie, but you can call me *Mammi.* I'm so happy to meet you."

"Are you really my *grossmammi?*"

His mother's eyes brightened. "So your father has taught you some Pennsylvania Dutch. That's *goot.*"

"He didn't teach me. Leah taught me."

He caught the worried glance his mother flashed him. "You have spoken with Leah?"

"We met in town." He looked down at his daughter. "She's looking forward to having Joy come to her school."

"Leah is a kind woman. Your brother and his wife are inside. I thought you should know that."

He shoved his hands in his pockets. "Then it really is a family reunion."

"I have not told Wayne that you are returning. He doesn't know about Joy, either."

"Did you tell Father?"

"Ja."

Caleb straightened and took Joy by the hand. "Then we should go in."

His mother nodded and walked quickly back to the house. He followed more slowly. As they reached the door, Wayne blocked their way. A thunderous expression darkened his face. "There is nothing here for you. Go back where you came from."

"Wayne, please." Maggie's gaze darted between her sons.

"Shame on you, Mother. How could you do this to us? Rhonda, David, we are going home." He stood aside. His wife and son hurried out the door. The boy stared at Caleb with wide, curious eyes. Rhonda didn't even look. She kept her face down as she rushed past him, one hand covering her scarred cheek. Wayne followed close behind them.

Caleb caught his brother's arm and pulled him to a stop. He whispered, "Have you told her the truth?"

Wayne pushed him away. "There is nothing to tell. You are not welcome."

Caleb stepped aside. Joy clung to his leg, hiding her face. He placed a reassuring hand on her head. "Wayne, can we at least be civil to each other? For Mother's sake if not for our own."

Wayne stood at the gate as his wife and son climbed in the buggy. "'Be ye not unequally yoked together with unbelievers: for what fellowship hath righteousness with unrighteousness? And what communion hath light with darkness?' *2 Corinthians* 6:14."

"I remember the passage."

"Do not trouble me or mine. We do not know you."

With that, he strode to the buggy, climbed in and quickly drove away.

"What did you expect, Maggie?" Caleb's father asked from the doorway. "You should have told them Caleb was coming. You should have given them a chance to prepare."

"*Mamm* didn't know I would arrive today."

"I planned to tell Wayne and Rhonda tonight, that's why I asked them to come over, but then it was too late. Caleb was already here."

Ike stepped back from the door. "Come inside. We're letting all the heat out."

Maggie went in. Caleb picked up Joy and followed her. His father closed the door behind them.

The warmth of the kitchen was a welcome relief from the chill outside. The smell of the evening meal lingered in the air. His mother had been baking bread. There were five loaves lined up on the counter. The delicious aroma was enough to make Caleb's stomach rumble. Three animal crackers didn't make for a substantial supper.

Ike looked at Joy. "Who have we here?"

Caleb braced himself. "This is my daughter, Joy."

"And where is your wife?"

He met his father's steely look without flinching. "I'm not married."

Ike's lips thinned with displeasure. He gathered himself and managed a smile for Joy. "Welcome to our home, Joy. I'm Ike Mast, your *daadi,* your grandfather."

She looked at Caleb and whispered, "Is he like Nana's Jake?"

"No, honey, he's your real grandfather. He's much nicer than Jake."

Caleb set her down. She gave Ike a tentative smile. "Your house smells good."

He chuckled. "I reckon it's your grandma's cooking that smells good. Are you hungry?"

She nodded. He tipped his head toward the large wooden table. "Have a seat and Maggie will fix you something to eat."

"You mean *Mammi*," she corrected him as she climbed on a chair.

"*Ja,* your *mammi.* You know some of our speech. That is *goot.* Good."

"What is *ja?*"

"*Ja* means yes," Caleb explained.

"*Ja* is yes. Good is *goot.*" Joy nodded vigorously, making her straight blond hair swish across her face. She pressed it back with both hands.

Ike looked Caleb up and down. He nodded toward the table. "You look like you could use some of your mother's cooking. You're skin and bones."

The tension holding Caleb upright drained away, leaving him weak and shaken. To be invited to sit at the table with his father was more than he'd hoped for. He had to clear his throat of a lump the size of Texas before he could speak. *"Danki."*

Joy held out her hand. "Sit by me, Daddy."

Maggie was grinning widely. "He can't, child. This is the women's side of the table. He must sit across from us. I will sit by you as soon as I get some food on. Husband, would you like something?"

"A slice of your fresh bread with butter."

"*Kaffi,* too?"

"*Ja.*"

As his mother went to the counter and began cutting a loaf of bread, Caleb rounded the table and pulled out the chair on his father's right-hand side.

He had almost forgotten how fully Amish traditions permeated every aspect of life. His father sat at the head of the table, with his wife on his left. Sons sat on his right-hand side, from youngest to oldest down the table; daughters

sat beside their mother in the same fashion. Caleb knew without a doubt that his chair had been empty since he left home. An empty chair was a pointed reminder to everyone about who was missing.

"Bread and butter will be fine for me, too, *Mamm,* but no coffee."

"Lemonade, then?"

"Sure." She wouldn't be satisfied until she had made a special effort to please him. If he let her, she would cook a feast. It was late, but he knew that tomorrow mounds of food would be set in front of him. Cooking was his mother's way of showing her love.

She soon had thick slices of fresh baked bread slathered with peanut-butter spread for Joy, and butter for him and his father. She gave Ike his coffee and Joy a mug of milk, then she set two glasses of lemonade on the table. Still smiling, she took a seat beside Joy.

Her hand shook slightly as she tucked a strand of Joy's hair behind her ear. "I have wanted a granddaughter for a very long time. I am so happy that *Gott* brought you to us."

Joy gave her a beaming peanut-butter-smeared smile. "Daddy said you would like me. I like you, too. I had another *mammi.* I called her Nana. She went to heaven."

"I'm sorry to hear that. You must miss her. She is with *Gott* now, so we must be happy for her."

"Who is *Gott?*" Joy asked around a mouthful of bread.

"God," Caleb translated.

"Tomorrow, you can tell me all about her. It's getting late. It's time for a little one like you to be in bed," Maggie said.

"Can I sleep here?"

Maggie nodded. "I have a room upstairs that's just for you. Finish your bread and your milk. I will show you the way."

Caleb rose from his place and headed for the door. "I'll get our suitcases."

Outside, he paused to watch his breath fog in the cold evening air. He missed the warmth of the Gulf breezes. He'd forgotten how hard the cold could bite his face and make his eyes water. How long would he have to stay? How soon would Joy adjust to life among the Amish? Would she adjust? Was he expecting too much? Even with Leah to help guide her, it was going to be a difficult transition.

Hunching against the cold, he hurried down the steps and gathered enough of their things to make it through the night. Tomorrow would be soon enough to unpack the rest.

He unplugged his cell phone from the car charger and put it in his pocket. His truck battery would be the only source of electricity for keeping his phone charged while he stayed on the farm. His parents wouldn't like the fact that he was bringing a phone into their home, but he needed it to maintain contact with his attorney.

Back in the house, he saw his mother had already taken Joy from the room. His father was sitting quietly at the table. A troubled frown marred his brow. "I'm afraid to ask because I think I know the answer, but I must hear it from you. Are you here to stay, *sohn?*"

"*Nee, Daed.* Only for a while."

"It breaks your mother's heart to see your place at the table empty."

"Perhaps having Joy here will ease some of her pain."

"Your child cannot heal what is broken in this family."

"I'm sorry. I couldn't stay."

"We have forgiven you. Rhonda has forgiven you. Wayne will forgive you in time."

"That would be nice if there was anything to forgive. I'm not the father of Rhonda's child. I don't know who is, but it isn't me."

"Why would Rhonda maintain such a lie?"

"I wish I knew. I wish that you believed me."

His father's frown deepened. "You come to my door with another child born out of wedlock and ask that I believe you are innocent?"

"I knew there'd be no point going through this again. Look, Joy needs a stable family life. She hasn't had that. I can't give it to her. I'm hoping you can. I know it's asking a lot, but will you consider raising her?"

His father was silent so long that Caleb started to think the whole trip had been for nothing.

"You think her life will be better, will be happier, with us but without you, her father?"

Leah had asked him the same thing. "I hope so."

"Where is the child's mother now?"

"I have no idea. She went out to smoke a cigarette and never came back. I turned the city upside down looking for her."

"Then you understand a little of what we felt when you left."

Facing the truth was hard. Caleb saw his actions in a different light now. "I admit I didn't go about leaving in the best way, but I felt it was my only option."

Ike banged his hand on the table. "Running away from a problem never fixes it."

"Some problems can't be fixed!" Caleb struggled to control his temper. This was his father. Ike deserved respect.

"Can't I leave you two alone for ten minutes without an argument starting?" Caleb's mother asked from the doorway.

"It wasn't an argument," Ike said gruffly.

She gave him a sympathetic look. "We all need a good night's sleep. In the morning, things will look different."

No, they wouldn't, but Caleb didn't say that. Ike rose from the table and went through the door that led to their living room and their bedroom beyond.

Maggie came and stood in front of Caleb. "I am so pleased that you are here. I'm glad, too, that you have brought this child with you."

"I didn't know what else to do. I didn't come back to make trouble."

She laid a hand on his cheek. "All of life is made up of bits of happiness and bits of trouble. In between, there is prayer and hard work and if we are blessed, sometimes wondrous joy. This is the way of the world."

"All struggle and no reward," he said dryly.

"Our rewards come in God's own time. You need rest. I see how weary you are. I made up the bed in your old room. Joy is waiting for her nightclothes in the bedroom over the kitchen."

"Thanks." Without central heat, the room over the kitchen was always the warmest one on the second story. He picked up their bags and started toward the stairs.

"Caleb?"

He glanced over his shoulder, waiting for his mother to say more. She hesitated, then said, "Don't be too hard on your father. He doesn't know how to bend without breaking. The two of you are more alike than you think."

He nodded. "I was wrong not to keep in touch. A card once a year wasn't enough, was it?"

Tears filled her eyes. "It wasn't enough, but it gave me joy every Christmas to know that you were all right and thinking of me."

"I'll do better in the future. I promise."

A frown creased her brow. "You will not be staying?"

He heard the pain in her voice, but she deserved the truth. "Only for a while."

Tears filled her eyes. She dabbed at them with the corner of her apron. The last thing Caleb wanted was to upset her. "I'm sorry. I came because I want the two of you to raise Joy. I know what I'm asking won't be easy. I will help

financially, so you don't have to worry about that. I have a good job, but it takes me away from home a lot. I may even be leaving the country soon."

Maggie shook her head. "It is not about the money."

"I know that. Will you consider my request?"

"How long can you say?"

He noticed she hadn't given him an answer. She wouldn't. It would be his father's decision.

"Until I'm certain that this is the right move for Joy."

She came and cupped his face between her hands. "Then I will treasure every minute and pray you have a change of heart."

"That's not likely."

"*Ach,* but it is not impossible. *Gott* may yet answer my prayers."

Chapter Five

Early the following morning, Caleb dressed quickly in his room, having slept better than he had in years. There was something comforting about huddling under a mound of quilts in a chilly room. However, getting dressed in the cold was a good reminder of why he liked living in the South. He might need to invest in a couple pairs of long johns. Joy would need some for sure.

He checked on her and found her bed empty. He rushed downstairs in a panic. Thankfully, she was seated at the kitchen table, enjoying scrambled eggs, bacon, biscuits and fried potatoes. The aroma of his mother's cooking made his mouth water and his stomach rumble.

Mamm came in from the other room. "Ah, *goot,* you are up. I must go into town and get some fabric for Joy's new dresses. I'd best hurry if I'm to get there and back in time to fix your *daed* his lunch. There is a plate in the *offa* for you."

"That means oven," Joy said with a grin. She had a streak of his mother's homemade apple butter smeared on her cheek.

He winked at her. *"Mien meiya eems es in da offa."*

Her eyes widened. "You speak Pennsylvania Dutch?"

"Pretty *goot, ja?*"

"What did you say?" she demanded.

"I said, 'My morning meal is in the oven.'"

"That is...way cool."

He had finally impressed his eight-year-old daughter. The morning was looking up.

His mother moved to stand behind Joy. She stroked her hair with a look of tenderness in her eyes. "Finish your breakfast. Your *daed* can teach you many words while he shows you around the farm today."

"Okay." Joy started forking eggs in her mouth. It was the first time he'd seen his child relaxed in weeks. His mother and her comfort food had that effect on people. It was exactly what he wanted for Joy.

Caleb used a hot pad to pull his heaping plate from the oven. After he finished his breakfast, he made sure Joy was well bundled up in a new coat, snow boots and mittens they had purchased on their way north. Together, they set off along the same path he had used countless times when he walked to school. It felt familiar and strange. Joy ran in front of him, kicking up clouds of powdery fresh snow that had fallen in the night.

As they got deeper into the woods, she drew close to him and took his hand. "I don't think I like this place."

"You don't like the woods?" He tried to see their surroundings through the eyes of a child who had grown up in a run-down trailer park on the outskirts of Houston. The two places were worlds apart. Trees pressed in around them. The bare branches creaked and clacked in the cold breeze.

"I think something might get us," she whispered, her hesitant voice wobbled with fear.

"I walked through these woods every day from the time I was your age until I was grown. I never saw anything that could get me. Shall we check and see who else has walked along this path?"

"How can we do that?"

"Everyone who walked this way or crossed this path

has left their signature in the snow. Turn around and look where we've walked. What do you see?"

She stopped and looked back. "I see our footprints."

"That's right. Now look in front of us. What do you see?"

She scanned the area. "I see funny marks in the snow."

"Let's take a closer look." He crouched beside the dots that crossed the path in front of them.

She imitated his position and propped her chin on her hand. He almost laughed at her serious expression but quickly controlled himself. It was important that she learn to be at home in the outdoors. "If you look closely, you'll see two tiny paw marks in the snow and two drag marks behind it."

She looked up at him. "Are they puppy tracks?"

"That's a good guess. Puppies have little feet, but this was made by someone who hops along."

Her eyes grew round. "A rabbit?"

"That's right."

She jumped up and rushed toward the edge of the path. "Can I see it?"

He caught her by the shoulder. "Whoa. We might see a rabbit later, but we can't follow him. We have to stick to the path."

"Why?"

"Because rushing into the woods without knowing your way around is how you get lost. You must never do that. Let's keep walking and see who else has shared our path."

She gazed longingly toward the rabbit tracks but allowed herself to be led away. After a few dozen yards, she pointed ahead of them. "I see more tracks, Daddy. Who made those?"

"Those were made by a big deer. Can you see how they are split in two and pointed?"

She ran ahead of him and stopped, pointing at her feet. "Who made these?"

"That's the footprints of a raccoon. See how the paw marks are like little handprints? Mr. Raccoon has hands a lot like you and I for gripping things. He has a face like a bandit with a black mask around his eyes and a short snout with sharp little teeth."

She took a step back and pulled her hands to her chin. "Does he bite?"

"He would bite you if you tried to pick him up. If you let him mind his business, he will let you mind yours and everyone will stay happy."

"Did you walk to school by yourself? Grandpa says I'll have to learn to walk to school by myself. When I'm grown up I can drive a buggy."

So his father was considering letting Joy live with them. "You won't have to go by yourself until you feel good about doing it. I didn't walk alone. I walked with my brother until he got too old for school."

"Uncle Wayne? I don't like him."

His first impulse was to say that he didn't like Wayne, either, but he held his tongue. He loved his brother. He didn't like the way things had turned out between them. Joy was going to be living here. She would have to learn to get along with everyone in the family.

"Your uncle Wayne can seem gruff, but he is a good man. I think you will come to like him in time. His little boy is almost the same age as you."

They heard the sound of crashing in the underbrush. Joy threw her arms around his leg and held on tight. "What's that?"

They had their answer as a black-and-white dog bounded out of the woods and came loping toward them. Caleb's heart gave a glad leap when he thought it was Trixie, but he quickly saw he was mistaken. This dog shared similar markings but was taller and heavier with more brown on his legs.

"Duncan won't hurt you." They both turned as Leah walked up beside them.

Caleb hadn't forgotten that she and Rhonda used to take the same shortcut through the woods on their way to school. Had he subconsciously come this way in the hopes of meeting her? Maybe.

In any case, he was pleased to see her again. Very pleased.

"Leah!" Joy shouted and waved.

"Hello." She smiled brightly at his child.

The tug of attraction was strong, but it was foolish to dwell on it. He'd be leaving in a few weeks. Still, something about her made the morning brighter. If things had been different, if they had met in another time and another place, he would have followed the urge to know her better, but she wasn't for him.

To her, he was an outsider. The man who'd dishonored and abandoned her sister. He should be thankful she had taken an interest in helping Joy.

"I'm so happy to see you." Joy ran to her and wrapped her arms around Leah's legs. Duncan joined the game and jumped up, too. The impact of the child and the big dog together knocked the teacher off balance. Caleb lunged forward to catch her.

Leah staggered into Caleb. His strong arms closed around her and kept her upright, saving her from a tumble in the snow.

She looked up and saw a slow smile curve his lips. Her heart skittered wildly for an instant before she remembered who was holding her. Struggling to regain her composure, she moved away from him.

"I wasn't expecting to see you this morning." Her voice sounded breathless. She stopped talking and pressed her lips together.

Caleb thrust his hands in his coat pockets. "Joy and I

are exploring. So this is the proud papa." He bent to scratch Duncan behind one ear.

"He showed up outside my door today. I guess he knew something was up."

"Did he like Pickles?" Joy asked.

"*Ja.* He looked over the litter, and I think he liked Pickles a lot. Trixie normally walks with me to school in the mornings, but she's too busy with her puppies. Duncan occasionally joins us."

Joy was still hanging on to her leg. "Does he bite?"

"Never," Leah assured her in all seriousness. "Duncan, sit."

The dog promptly sat. "Now shake hands with Joy."

He raised his paw. Joy let go of Leah's leg and tentatively shook the dog's front paw. Duncan added a quick lick to Joy's fingers, making her squeal.

"Did you see that, Daddy? He kissed my hand."

"I saw. He's a very polite pooch."

"It was nice seeing you again, Joy. I must be going. The teacher can't be late to school. Come, Duncan." There was always plenty to be done before her students arrived.

"I thought I would show Joy the way to the school. Mind if we walk with you?" Caleb waited for her reply, watching her intently.

"Of course not." She had to be polite, didn't she?

"Duncan's owner must not live far away," Caleb said.

"He belongs to Carl King. He works for Joseph Shetler on his sheep farm just over the next hill."

"I remember Woolly Joe, but I don't remember a man named King."

"Carl is a newcomer. He has *Englisch* ways, but some people wonder if he isn't ex-Amish from another place. He and Woolly Joe keep to themselves. I think Duncan enjoys visiting the school for a dose of company."

Joy, more confident now, ran ahead a little ways with

the dog dancing at her heels. The path was wide enough for a few hundred yards, but it narrowed, forcing Leah and Caleb closer together. The bare branches of the trees laced together overhead and gave Leah the feeling of being sheltered. Snow crunched under their boots. Occasional clumps of it fell from the trees and scattered in the breeze, leaving sparkling showers in their wake. It was a beautiful morning. Caleb walked close beside her in silence.

She glanced at him and wondered what he was thinking. His gaze was on Joy and the dog. A sweet smile curved his lips. It would be good for both of them if he changed his mind and stayed, even if he didn't give up his *Englisch* ways. Could Leah help him see that?

Joy stopped and pointed to the ground. "I see more rabbit tracks."

He squatted beside her. "You're right. A rabbit went this way not long ago. Keep your eyes peeled for more tracks."

Joy patted Duncan's head and grinned at Leah. "Daddy is teaching me about animal tracks. This is a rabbit track, and I know a raccoon track and people tracks and now I know dog tracks. Duncan is making big tracks in the snow."

The dog had his nose down investigating the new trail. After a few seconds, he took off at a trot back the way they had come.

Joy frowned. "Where's he going?"

"Home, I reckon," Leah said.

Joy's frown turned into a pout. "I wish he would stay with me. I miss him."

Caleb lifted her chin so she would look at him. "He has work to do. If you ask Leah very nicely, she might let you visit Trixie and her puppies again after school one of these days."

Joy's beaming smile returned. "Could I? Please?"

"I'd like that," Leah replied and spared a sidelong glance at Caleb. He wasn't as she had imagined him all these years.

He wasn't indifferent to his child or harsh. She had pictured him living in a perpetual *rumspringa,* doing all that was forbidden to the Amish, drinking, going to parties and movies and driving fast cars.

What had his life been like? And why did it matter? If only she could quell her curiosity about him. As they kept walking, she tried, but it seemed that she couldn't give up the need to know more. She finally blurted out, "What kind of work do you do in Texas?"

He seemed surprised by her question. She was a little surprised herself at her boldness.

"I'm a roughneck. I work on oil rigs, mostly off-shore rigs. The pay is better."

"Out in the ocean?" Her secret dream had always been to travel. To see the mountains and the oceans, to view and admire God's handiwork beyond the hills and fields of her small community.

"Yes, out in the ocean or rather in the Gulf of Mexico."

"Was it wonderful? Was it frightening?"

"Mostly it was noisy, hard work for very long hours. At times, it could be too beautiful for words. Then again, during some bad storms, I only wanted to get my feet back on dry land."

"To look upon the ocean must be a wondrous thing." She couldn't help the longing that slipped into her tone.

"You should go."

She looked down. "I have no reason for such a journey."

"Travel isn't forbidden. Many Amish visit the seashore."

"I couldn't go alone, and I don't know of anyone who would go with me." Outside of her friend Levi Beachy, she hadn't spoken to anyone who wished to see more of the world the way she did. Levi had planned to move to an Amish settlement in Colorado, but then he had married her friend Sarah and they were both happy to remain in Hope Springs now.

"Don't some of the older couples around here travel to Florida for the winter? I've heard it's a popular destination for Amish snowbirds."

"Some do. Not many."

"If the chance comes up, you should go along."

"I teach school through the winter, so that won't work."

"I guess not, but you won't always be teaching."

"True. Someday I'll be too old to keep up with the children."

"The ocean will still be there for you."

She hadn't expected him to be understanding and sympathetic. Under other circumstances, he was the kind of man she could like.

Caleb was sorry when they arrived at the school. For a while, he had forgotten that he didn't belong here. Leah was responsible for that. He wanted to ask if she had found forgiveness in her heart for him, but he knew it didn't matter. He would leave again anyway.

She went ahead of him up the steps. He and Joy followed her into the school building. Immediately, the smells and the sight of the interior filled him with nostalgia. Nothing had changed in the years he'd been gone.

The floor was the same wide planking, scuffed but clean. Light poured in from the large windows along both sides of the single room. A blackboard covered two thirds of the front wall. Above it, student artwork was still displayed. The childish drawings were much the same, even if they had been done by different hands.

Squarely in the middle of the front sat a large stove. It could burn wood or coal, depending on how much heat the building needed. Slightly off to one side was Leah's desk. Books and stacks of papers were arranged neatly on the shelves behind it. Old-fashioned wooden student

desks were arranged in four rows, two on either side of a wide center aisle.

He could remember hiding behind the open lid of his desk near the back and sharing a laugh with his friends. The teacher would eventually come by and silence their conversation with a pointed look. Lidia Yoder had been a stern but fair teacher who had no trouble quelling the occasional rowdy student.

"What happened to Lidia Yoder? Is she still around?"

"She lives in a little house in Hope Springs. You should go see her."

"I might do that."

He tried to remember where Leah sat in the old days, but he couldn't recall. He hadn't had his eye on girls at that stage of his life. Mostly, he'd wanted to be out playing Duck, Duck, Goose, softball or sledding when the snow was deep enough.

Leah went straight to the stove and opened the firebox door. It was the teacher's job to arrive early and get the stove going so the room would be warm by the time the children arrived. He said, "I'll bring in some coal for you."

"*Danki.* That would be nice. I'll get the kindling ready."

He picked up a large black metal bucket from the side of the stove. His daughter had gone to gaze at the blackboard. "Joy, why don't you come with me? I'll show you the coal shed."

She picked up a piece of chalk from the tray that ran the length of blackboard. "Can I draw instead?"

He glanced at Leah. She nodded. He said, "Sure. Just do what Leah tells you. I'll be back in a few minutes."

Suddenly, Joy spun around, a worried look on her face. "Promise you'll come back?"

His heart contracted painfully. That was exactly what her mother had done. Said she'd be back in a minute and then pulled her disappearing act. He crossed the room and

dropped to one knee in front of Joy. He knew Leah was listening although she pretended to be busy with the stove. "Honey, I promise I won't ever leave without telling you where I'm going and when to expect me back. Okay?"

"Okay." She didn't sound convinced, but the panic was gone from her eyes.

"Good."

"You mean *goot*."

Grinning, he nodded. "*Ja, goot.* Can you draw me a picture of Pickles?"

"Okay. How do you say *dog* in Pennsylvania Dutch?"

"*Hund.*" He stood and picked up his bucket.

"How do you say *cats?*"

He was already halfway to the door. "*Katz.*"

"Daddy, that's the same."

"Many of our words are the same or very similar," Leah said. "In school, my students only speak English, while at home they speak Pennsylvania Dutch. While you are trying to learn our language, I am teaching my students your language."

"That's just weird." Joy turned back to the board and made a large oval.

Caleb paused in the open door. "She has a point. It is weird."

He ducked outside before Leah could reply, but he caught a glimpse of her engaging grin before he closed the door.

Wouldn't it be nice if he could make her smile more often?

Chapter Six

"**W**hy are we stopping, Daddy?"

Late on Sunday morning, Caleb parked his truck at the end of the lane leading to the Sutter farm. The three-hour service would be ending soon.

He hadn't wanted Joy to spend the entire time sitting on a hard bench and listening to preaching in a language she couldn't understand. Not yet. He wanted to expose her gradually to the things an Amish life would include. Bringing her late to the preaching was a step along that path, although he knew not everyone would approve.

"I'm stopping here because it wouldn't be polite to arrive at a church meeting in an *Englisch* vehicle."

"Why?"

"Because Amish people come to the church services on foot or in a buggy."

"Why?"

He sighed heavily and repeated the phrase he'd heard a hundred times during his childhood when he questioned why things were done. "Because that is the way it has always been."

"Okay."

Surprisingly, the answer was enough for her. It hadn't been for him. She pushed open the door on her side and

stepped out. He reluctantly joined her. An Amish Sunday service was the last place he wanted to be. Maybe he should have let her come with his folks. He would have been home when she came back.

This time.

Thinking about the day he wouldn't be around when she came home made him squirm. He couldn't stay. His life wasn't here, but Joy's could be. He had to keep what was best for her at the forefront of his mind and not dwell on how much he was going to miss having her around. She appeared to be settling in well with his parents. Much better than he had expected. She hadn't pitched a fit or talked about her mother in days.

She held open her jacket and made an awkward twirl in front of him. "Do you like my dress, Daddy? It's the very first dress I ever owned. *Mammi* made my dress and my *kapp*." She patted the white head covering that marked her as Amish.

"*Mammi* made me two white *kapps* and two black ones."

"You look very Plain in it, honey."

She scowled and stared at the ground. "I know I'm not pretty like other girls."

His heart twisted with pain. She'd never been made to feel good about herself. He crouched in front of Joy and smoothed the creases from her white apron. "Looking Plain means you look very Amish. The blue color of your dress makes your eyes as bright as the sky."

"I'm still ugly."

He lifted Joy's chin with his finger. "Never think that. God made you pretty in a very special way. He made you pretty from the inside out, not just on the outside like some girls."

She looked up with uncertainty in her eyes. "He did?"

"Yes, He did. Do you know what I see when I look at

you? I see the prettiest girl in the whole world wearing a brand-new dress made by a grandmother who loves her."

Her frown vanished. "And a new *eahmal shatzli*."

It meant *long apron,* and it was part of a young Amish girl's traditional dress. "Someday, when you are grown-up enough, you will put off wearing your long apron and wear a matching cape and short apron like your grandmother."

It was a huge milestone in an Amish girl's life. Another one he wouldn't be around to see. The thought brought a funny ache to his chest.

Joy held her apron out and flapped it. "I don't have to take it off today, do I?"

He smiled. "No, not today. Today, you're going to your first Amish church service in your brand-new dress."

"I hear singing, Daddy."

"I hear it, too." The slow cadence of Amish voices rose and fell as each word was drawn out over several notes. There was no music, only voices raised in worship.

"I don't know that song. It sounds sad."

He knew it by heart. He'd sung it countless times while seated on hard wooden benches, eager to have the service end so he could get out and visit with his friends and get up a game of volleyball or horseshoes.

"No one expects you to know it, Joy. You will learn that song in time, and many the other songs, too. Are you ready to go?"

"Yes. I mean, *ja*."

"*Ja* is *goot*."

She pressed her hands to her mouth and giggled. "You sound just like grandpa when you speak Amish, Daddy."

"Do I? I reckon that's not a bad thing." He deeply admired his father. If only the feeling could be mutual.

They walked up the dirt drive, taking care to avoid the slushy snow melting in the sunshine. When they reached the house, he stopped and looked down at Joy. "Amish men

and women don't sit together at the preaching. You will have to go in and find your grandmother."

"Aren't you coming in?"

"No." He wouldn't be welcome. Wayne would have seen to that. In a way, he felt sorry for his brother. It couldn't be easy living with so much guilt and fear.

"What if I can't find Grandma?"

"You will, but if you don't see her, it's okay to ask where she is. You'll have to sit still and be quiet until the service is over, but then you can play with the other kids and there will be lots to eat."

"What if the other kids don't like me?"

"They will. But if you want, you can stay with your grandmother, okay?"

"I guess."

"Go on inside."

"You won't go away and leave me here, will you?"

She couldn't shake the fear of being left alone. Who could blame her? He pointed to a stump by the corral fence. "I'll be waiting right over there."

"Promise?"

"I promise."

She studied him for a long moment, trying to decide if he was telling the truth, then she nodded and walked up the steps and inside the house. He waited by the door, expecting her to come running back out, but she remained inside. It was a small victory for him and for her.

Half an hour later, the final hymn faded away and Caleb knew the service had ended. He waited out at the stump with his hands pushed deep in his coat pockets. It was sunny but still cold. He saw Joy come out with his mother. Joy darted across the yard toward him.

"I was good, Daddy. I sat real still, and I prayed for you because *Mammi* said I should."

If God listened to anyone, surely He would listen to this child. "Thank you. I'm glad you were good."

"Don't you mean *danki?*"

"I do. *Danki* for your prayers." Caleb lifted a hand to wave to his mother and let her know he would keep Joy with him. She nodded and went back inside to help prepare for the meal.

Caleb saw his brother come out with their father. He met their gazes before they both turned away without acknowledging him. It hurt to be ignored in front of others, but he steeled himself to endure it. He hadn't taken the vows of baptism, but his actions, so far outside of what was expected of an Amish person, made his presence unacceptable to many.

Joy was chattering about the funny man with a beard who spoke during church when Caleb caught sight of Leah as she came out with her sister. Rhonda saw him and quickly averted her eyes. She pulled at Leah's arm, but Leah ignored her. In front of everyone, she crossed the yard toward him.

Leah knew what she was doing would set tongues wagging, but she didn't want Joy to see her father being ostracized by everyone in her new community. He'd made the effort to bring his daughter to church. Leah reluctantly admired his courage in doing so. If only he had found the courage to marry her sister instead of running away from his responsibilities all those years ago. All their lives would have been different.

And Joy wouldn't be among them.

The child ran to greet her. "Leah, I didn't see you inside."

She smiled at the child, so full of happiness today. "I was there. I saw how well behaved you were."

"Danki."

Leah let her smile fade as she looked at Caleb. "Good morning."

"You mean *guter mariye,*" Joy said with a bright smile. She was such a charming child. She seemed eager to learn all things Amish.

"Are you sure you know what you're doing?" Caleb stared past Leah. She knew all eyes were on them.

"I wanted to ask if you were able to get Joy's school records."

"I had my attorney fax them to the local public library, since I don't have access to a printer. I picked them up yesterday. They're in the truck. I left it parked at the end of the lane."

She hesitated. Walking off with him alone, even for a short trip, would put her in a tenuous position.

He seemed to sense her reluctance. He gestured toward the highway. "I'll go get them. Would you look after Joy until I get back?"

"Of course."

"Joy, mind Leah. Would you like to go home with me or ride home in the buggy with *Mammi* and *Daadi?*"

She squeezed her eyes shut. "The buggy!"

His gaze remained on Leah. "I wouldn't trust her to just anyone, but I've seen how well you can handle her. I'll be back in a few minutes. Do you want a box of *a-n-i-m-a-l c-r-a-c-k-e-r-s?* I have some in my pocket just in case."

"We'll be fine." He trusted her to look after Joy. The thought filled her with warmth. She watched him walk away with long, sure strides.

And why shouldn't he trust her? Looking after children was what she did. Other people's children—never her own. Because of him.

She accepted it as God's will, but sometimes she wondered why she was the one left without love in her life. She loved her students and they loved her, but it wasn't the same.

That love couldn't hold her with tender arms or kiss away her fears in the darkness. She longed for the things marriage would bring—companionship, shared laughter, a sense of belonging to something important. But it wasn't to be.

Rhonda came up to stand at her side. "You shouldn't be talking to him."

"He isn't under the ban. We have no cause to shun him."

"How can you say that?"

Leah gave a tiny shake of her head and glanced toward Joy. This wasn't a conversation the child should hear. Fortunately, Anna Imhoff came up to greet Joy. "Anna, why don't you take Joy and introduce her to some of the other children?"

As they walked away, Leah turned to her sister. "It happened a long time ago. Nothing can change it. Maybe it's time to forgive Caleb."

"I have forgiven him, but I'd rather you didn't talk to him."

"He wishes to enroll his daughter in our school."

"Is he staying in Hope Springs?" Panic flooded Rhonda's face.

"No. He knows the school board must agree to allow Joy to attend Walnut Valley. I told him what records we would need. I owe Caleb the same attention I owe any parent. Nothing more."

"I wish he would leave and be done with it. Is he eager to rid himself of his daughter?"

"I don't think he is eager to leave her." She sensed a conflict in him. Was it because he didn't want to leave his child or because he didn't want to leave her with his Amish family?

Rhonda huffed. "I see. You've taken one of your broken-winged fancies to him, haven't you?"

"I haven't taken a fancy to him. I have taken a fancy to his daughter. Joy can be a trial, but she has a big heart."

"She'll be better off without him."

"I think they belong together." Joy needed her father in her life. And maybe her father needed her more than he knew.

Maggie came out of the house. She stopped short and looked around with a worried frown. "Leah, did Caleb leave?"

"*Nee.* He will be back in a few minutes."

"Where is Joy?"

Leah pointed toward the barn. "She is playing with Anna and meeting the other children."

Maggie relaxed. "That's fine. I want her to make friends."

"Speaking of friends, that reminds me. Did Rhonda tell you I'm having a cookie-baking frolic at my house on Wednesday evening?"

"I forgot to mention it," Rhonda said quickly. She stared at her feet. "So much has happened."

Leah and Maggie shared a sympathetic glance. They knew Caleb's return had been hard on Rhonda. Leah tried to lighten the mood. "You're welcome to come, Maggie, and bring Joy, too. I'm sure she would enjoy that."

"I'm not sure, but thank you for the invitation. I'd better get back inside and help Nettie clear plates so the next group can eat. It was good of you to let Bishop Zook know the Chupp family is struggling. The community will make sure they have all they need until William is back on his feet."

"I noticed some bare cupboards when I visited them on a school matter. I did nothing special."

Maggie hesitated, glancing between Rhonda and Leah. "I must thank you, too, for being kind to Caleb and to Joy. You've made a good impression on the child."

"She is sweet."

"She truly is." Maggie went back inside.

Leah placed a hand on her sister's shoulder. "It's going to be okay."

"I don't see how. Maggie wants Caleb to stay. I can't imagine facing him at every family gathering, every church or school function."

When Caleb came back into sight, Rhonda pressed her hand to her scarred cheek and hurried inside the house. Leah waited until he approached. He looked after her sister. "I'm sorry my being here upsets Rhonda."

"Do you blame her?"

"That is a loaded question I choose not to answer. Here are Joy's records." He handed over a manila envelope. "*Danki*. I must get back to the house."

He frowned slightly, as if he were aware of her discomfort and knew he was the reason for it. He shoved his hands deep in his coat pockets. "Will you be at the school-board meeting?"

"I'll be there."

"Until Thursday, then."

She watched him walk back down the lane, with his shoulders hunched against the cold and against the stares that followed him. He looked so alone.

Leah wasn't surprised when her sister came over that evening. Although they made a habit of visiting each other at least once a month, the closeness they once shared was missing. Leah knew part of that was her fault.

"Do you know what you are doing?" Rhonda demanded.

"Good evening, Rhonda. Won't you at least let me take your coat before you start scolding me?"

"I can't stay. Why are you befriending Caleb Mast?"

"We talked about this at church. I don't believe I have befriended him. He wants to enroll his daughter in our school. She has special needs. It's important that I know what those are. I'm sure the school board will ask for my input on his request. I take my job seriously."

Rhonda paced the small kitchen. "I don't know why he had to come back."

Leah softened her tone. "He doesn't intend to stay long. He'll be gone and things will get back to normal, except Maggie and Ike will have another grandchild in school, and David will have a new cousin."

"I don't want David to have anything to do with Caleb or his *Englisch* daughter. Wayne won't tolerate it."

"I'm sorry he feels that way. Joy is a wonderful child who has led a very sad life. I think she can be happy here. I think she can learn our ways and become a productive member of our community. I hope he can see that. As a member of the school board, his acceptance of her is important."

"What if her father changes his mind and comes to take her away?"

"Is that what's wrong? Are you and Wayne afraid Caleb has come back to claim his son?"

"I wouldn't put it past him."

Leah drew her sister close. "He gave up any right to David when he denied him years ago. Wayne is David's father in every sense of the word."

"In every sense but one, and that is the most important."

"That is the least important part of being a father. Wayne loves David. He could not love him more if he tried."

"I know." Suddenly there were tears streaming down Rhonda's face. "But every time he sees my son he is reminded of my sin. I can tell by the way he looks at me. He can barely touch me. He is so angry now that Caleb is back. I don't know what to do."

Leah led her weeping sister to the sofa and sat beside her. She had always suspected that things weren't good between Rhonda and Wayne, but her sister had never spelled it out so plainly. Nor had Leah asked.

Rhonda looked up with pain-filled eyes. "You hate me, too."

"Oh, Rhonda, I don't hate you."

"I ruined everything for you."

"You did what you thought was best for you and your child."

"We don't talk like we used to. Remember when we were girls, we would huddle together under the quilts at home and talk about the boys we liked and the kind of lives we wanted to live? We used to laugh so much. We never laugh anymore."

Leah had been deeply hurt when Wayne broke their engagement to marry Rhonda. As the youngest child, Rhonda had always seemed to end up with the best of everything. She had been the prettiest girl in Hope Springs. Everyone said so. She was smarter, more popular, more outgoing—she was everything that Leah wasn't.

Rhonda could have told Wayne no. She could've gone to stay with their childless cousin in Indiana. The couple would have welcomed her and raised her baby as their own. It seemed to Leah that Rhonda was intent on spoiling her life, too, since she had ruined her own.

Leah had let her bitterness simmer, and it had tainted her relationship with her sister. It wasn't right.

"I remember how it was. We used to laugh all the time. You must come and stay with me for a few days. Wayne and David can manage without you. Who knows, Wayne may realize how much he misses you, for I believe he loves you, even if he has trouble showing it."

Rhonda pressed a hand to her scarred cheek. "If only I wasn't so ugly."

"You are not ugly, and you must never say so again. That is prideful and vain. We are all as God has made us, and we must accept that, flaws and all. True beauty shines from the heart, not from our faces."

"I try to accept it as God's will. You would think by now it wouldn't cross my mind, but I can't help how I feel."

Leah hesitated and chose her next words carefully. "Acceptance follows forgiveness. Have you forgiven Caleb for the accident that injured you?"

"Of course I have," she said quickly. Too quickly. There was no sincerity in her voice. "I just wish he would leave. It was better when he wasn't around." She started crying again. Leah held her tight and let her weep out her unhappiness.

The inability to find forgiveness was a trait both sisters shared. Leah thought about Caleb and Joy and about his struggle to do what was right for the child. He wasn't a cruel or careless man. Perhaps he hadn't been cruel and careless in the past. Maybe he had only been a frightened boy who couldn't face a man's responsibilities.

No matter what he had done or why, the Savior had died on the cross for his sins. Who was she to say it wasn't enough?

Caleb was at home when his parents returned with Joy late in the evening. He walked out to meet them.

Joy climbed out of the buggy. "I have a new friend, Daddy. Her name is Anna."

"That's good. Did you meet lots of new kids?"

"They didn't make fun of me, not even once."

"And why should they?" Ike asked as he helped Maggie out of the buggy.

"'Cause I'm not smart. I'm not good at games, and lots of times the kids call me stupid and other bad names."

The memory of such times took the light from his daughter's eyes. Caleb exchanged a speaking glance with his father. Maybe now he would understand why he had brought her here.

Ike pulled a large basket with handles from the backseat.

"There will be no name-calling from the children in our church. If this should happen, you must tell me at once so that I can speak to their parents. Now, take this inside and help your grandmother put our lunch things away.

Joy took the basket. It was almost bigger than she could manage. She hefted it higher and followed Maggie into the house.

Caleb took hold of the horse's bridle. "I'll put Bobby away."

To Caleb's surprise, his father didn't go inside. Instead, he stood by and watched as Caleb unhitched the black gelding. As he led the horse to his stall, his father followed and stood outside the pen. Once Caleb had unbuckled the bellyband and the collar, he lifted the harness off Bobby and set it on the boards.

Ike took it and hung it on the pegs made to hold it. "Your daughter seems to like it here. The place she came from, it sounds like she was unhappy there."

Caleb picked up a brush and began to rub down the horse. "I don't think Joy has met with much kindness in her life. Handicapped children are not always welcomed in the *Englisch* world. Some see them as a burden."

Ike stopped working and stared at Caleb. "And how do you see her?"

Chapter Seven

Caleb stopped brushing and looked over the animal's back at his father. "You mean do I see Joy as a burden?"

Ike began to wipe down the harness pieces with an oiled rag. "You bring her to us and say you intend to leave. What are we to think?"

"I'm sure it looks like I'm trying to get rid of her. I don't know. Maybe that is what I'm doing. I wasn't prepared to have a child, let alone one with Joy's special needs. I tried to manage, but the harder I tried the more difficult she became. She hid from me. She ran away. She kept trying to go back to where her grandmother lived because she thought her mother would come find her there. I lived in constant fear that she would disappear and I wouldn't be able to find her."

"This fear I know well. I have lived with it for many years."

Shame welled up in Caleb. "I have done some things that I'm not proud of in my life, but what I did to you and mother was cruel. I'm truly sorry. I hope you can forgive me."

"We forgave you long ago."

"*Danki,* Father. If Joy can't stay here with you, I don't know what I will do."

"Our ways are the best ways. *For us.*" He patted his chest

for emphasis. "They are not best for everyone. You have chosen an *Englisch* life. This I cannot like, but I know a man must find his own way. Until you are certain why you brought Joy to us, I cannot say that she may stay."

"You want to send her back into a world that is cruel and unjust to her?"

"It breaks my heart to say this, for she is flesh of my flesh, my own granddaughter, but you are her father. She belongs with you."

"You sound like Leah. I can't give Joy what she needs. She needs stability, a sense of belonging, a place where she can feel safe."

"What she needs, what all children need, is love. If you give her that, all else will follow."

Caleb started brushing Bobby again. "It's not always that simple."

"Which commandment did Jesus say was the first of all?"

"*Mark* 12:28–31. 'The first of all the commandments is, Hear, O Israel; The Lord our God is one Lord: And thou shalt love the Lord thy God with all thy heart, and with all thy soul, and with all thy mind, and with all thy strength: this is the first commandment. And the second is like, namely this, Thou shalt love thy neighbor as thyself. There is none other commandment greater than these.'"

Ike smiled. "You have not forgotten all I have taught you."

"No, not all."

Ike grew solemn again. "Your brother doesn't think I should allow you to stay here. He says you are unrepentant for the shame you brought on our family. Others in the church will agree with him."

"Good old Wayne. Always the upstanding one. The one that never got into trouble." He wasn't proud of the bitterness that seeped into his tone. Leah had said not every-

one had a forgiving nature. Like her, it was something he needed to work on.

Strange how often his thoughts turned to her and how much weight he gave to her words.

"You once looked at your brother with admiration and love, and he looked at you the same way. What came between the two of you?"

Caleb began putting away the grooming gear. "You know the story."

"I know what you both have told me. What haven't you told me?"

Caleb struggled with how to answer his father's question. The barn was quiet; only the rustling of the animals in the nearby stalls broke the stillness. As much as he wanted to clear his name and mend his relationship with his father, he couldn't do it. It wasn't his secret to share. He had given his promise to Wayne and he wouldn't go back on it.

"I wish I could tell you, *Daed,* but it's between Wayne and me. Can you accept that?"

"It seems that I must," Ike replied wearily.

"Do you want me to take my daughter and leave? I will. I don't want to cause trouble for you."

"What child doesn't cause a father trouble? *Nee,* you may stay awhile longer. Your mother hopes you will stay until Christmas, at least."

"I won't leave before then unless you ask me to."

"*Goot.* That will make your mother happy."

The two walked back to the house side by side. Ike stopped and looked up. "It will snow soon."

Caleb saw only clear blue sky. "Are your bones telling you that?"

"*Nee,* I heard the forecast on the radio at the feed store yesterday."

Chuckling, Caleb shook his head. "I've forgotten how

much of the outside world actually seeps into this community."

"As long as we do not seek the things of the outside world for ourselves but keep *Gott* at the front of our lives, there is little harm in listening to the radio once in a while."

"Especially when the Cleveland Indians are playing. How did they do this year?" His father, like a lot of Amish, loved baseball and followed local as well as national teams in the newspaper.

"Not as well as some, but there is always next year. Hope Springs had a *wunderbaar* girls' softball team this year. Those Miller twins can sure hit a ball. They went all the way to the state championships, but they didn't win. Reminded me of the time you and Wayne played for that team over by Berlin. You boys were *goot.* You made it to the state tournament, too."

"And we didn't win, either, but we had a great pitcher. Roman Weaver should have gone on to play pro ball. Is he still working with his *daed* at the sawmill?"

"*Nee,* Roman's arm was crushed when a car hit his buggy. He is slowly getting better, but he has taken over his uncle's printing business."

By this time, they had reached the house. Caleb held the door open for his father to go in. His mother was already at the stove getting started on supper. Joy knelt on a chair in front of the sink, washing the dishes they had brought home from lunch. She grinned at him. "Look, *Daed,* I'm helping."

"So you are." He'd never seen anyone so excited to be washing plates.

"Nana never let me wash dishes 'cause Jake said I was too clumsy. I only dropped one glass and broke it so far. *Mammi* didn't even get mad. She broke one, too."

"Did she?" Ike looked to his wife for an explanation.

Maggie shrugged. "I told her it could happen to anyone and not to fret. Then it happened to me. We are keeping

score. The one with the fewest broken dishes at the end of the year wins."

Ike huffed. "I reckon I'll be buying new plates before spring."

Maggie grinned. "A new set for Christmas would be nice. These are old and chipped. What were you two talking about?"

She was still hopeful that Caleb would change his mind and stay. He read it in her eyes.

Ike gave a slight shake of his head. She turned back to the stove, but her shoulders drooped ever so slightly.

"I was telling Caleb about Roman Weaver's accident."

Maggie stirred a pot of stew. "He sure surprised us all when he married Joann Yoder last month. I thought she would stay a spinster forever. Would you like some *kaffi,* Ike?"

He shook his head. "Maybe later. I think I'll read the Good Book for a while."

Joy slid off her chair. "I'm finished."

Ike looked over her work. "You've done a fine job. Would you like me to read you a story from the Bible?"

"I guess, since there isn't any TV."

Caleb slapped his palm over his mouth to keep from laughing out loud. His father scowled at him but extended his hand to Joy. "I will read you a story about a great flood and how *Gott* saved Noah and all the animals."

As his father and Joy left the kitchen, Caleb said, "I'll take a cup of coffee if you have it ready."

"Help yourself."

He fetched a mug from the cupboard and filled it from the pot simmering on the back of the stove. "Speaking of spinsters, I'm amazed that Leah never married."

He wasn't sure he should broach the subject, but his mother was in a position to know Leah pretty well.

"It wasn't from a lack of suitors. There were plenty of

young fellows who wanted to walk out with her, but she never took to anyone after…"

"After Wayne married Rhonda."

"Ja."

"She must have loved him a lot." Was it any wonder she hadn't forgiven Caleb for his part in wrecking her dreams of a home and a family of her own?

His mother turned to him. "All things happen for a reason, Caleb."

"I can't imagine the reason for so many messed-up lives." All because of him.

"Nor could I, but look into the other room. What do you see?"

He glanced over and saw his father in his favorite chair with Joy parked on his knee, listening intently as he read to her. "I see a little girl who is opening up, becoming the happy child I knew she could be."

"Ja. Gott sends such special children to a family for a special reason. He sent her to you. He has a reason. I, for one, am very, very grateful for His gift. You should be, too. Now, I must get some plums from the cellar. Your father loves to have plums for dessert on Sunday night." She opened the door at the back of the kitchen and took a lamp with her as she went downstairs.

Caleb sipped his coffee as he listened to the story his father was reading. He hadn't thought of Joy as a gift. He'd only seen the problems she presented. He was guilty of seeing her disability and not her abilities as surly as the people who'd made him angry when they looked away from her or called her retarded.

No more. From now on, he would focus on the positive things his daughter brought to him.

Coming here was meant to benefit Joy. It turned out that he was also reaping the benefits of his parents' wisdom and

faith. He had let an important part of himself wither away when he shut God out of his life.

A special child given for a special reason. Maybe his mother was right. Without Joy, he might never have come back to his family and to God.

He took his coffee into the living room and sat on the sofa next to his father and Joy. He listened to his father read the Bible and watched a whole new world open up for his child.

"I want to see the puppies. Pickles is missing me, I know she is. You don't want her to be unhappy, do you?"

Joy had been bugging Caleb for the past three days to visit Leah. He was running out of excuses. They were sitting on the back step, shelling black walnuts for his mother. She intended to bake black walnut cookies for an upcoming cookie exchange. The snow that had fallen on Sunday night was melting in the bright sunshine. His mother was doing her laundry at the propane-powered wringer washer on the back porch.

He cracked another shell and handed it to Joy to pick out the nut meat. "Honey, Leah may not be home."

"Call her and see."

"I can't call her. She doesn't have a phone. The Amish don't use telephones in their homes."

"That's just silly."

"It may seem silly to you, but it is not silly to Leah, or to grandpa and grandma. You can write her a letter and ask if you may come visit Pickles. In a few days you will have your answer."

"But I don't want to wait a few days. I want to see Pickles today."

"Not today. I'm sorry. I will help you write your letter." He was learning to be firm with her. She hadn't had a melt-

down since the one when they arrived in Hope Springs, but he knew it wouldn't take much to trigger another.

His mother came through the screen door with a basket of laundry in her arms. "Why the long face on such a beautiful day, Joy?"

"Daddy says I can't go see my puppy, and I'm sad."

Maggie looked to Caleb for an explanation. "Leah showed Joy her puppies the first day we came to town. She allowed Joy to name one. Since then, this kid has been bugging me to take her back to see them again."

"There's no reason you can't go visit Leah this evening."

A rush of eagerness filled Caleb at the thought of seeing Leah again. He was being foolish, but he couldn't help it. There was something special about her. It was more than the way she treated Joy. It was something he couldn't define. Simply being in her company made him happy. Did she feel the same way? Would she miss him when he was gone?

"Joy, can you help me hang the clothes on the line so they will dry?" his mother asked.

"Sure, but why don't you just put them in the dryer?"

Caleb put aside his hammer and followed them to the clothesline. Maggie set her basket down and raised her hands to the sky. "This is my clothes dryer. The good Lord has given me sunshine today. My clothes will be dry enough in no time. Didn't your Nana have a clothesline?"

"We took our things to the Laundromat."

"I think you will see that this way is better. The clothes will smell so nice and fresh. Can you help me pin these pants to the line?"

Joy stretched her arms above her head. "I can't reach it."

Caleb wrapped his arms around her waist and lifted her to the proper height. "Now can you get it?"

Joy giggled. "I'm as tall as you are."

"And almost as heavy. Get to pinning."

His arms were starting to ache by the time they were finished, but seeing his mother and his daughter working happily together was worth the discomfort.

When he put Joy's feet on the ground, she clapped her hands together and bounced up and down. "Can we go see the puppies now? Can we?"

His mother shook her head. "School doesn't let out until three-thirty. Then we must give Leah time to get home. You should go at four o'clock. I have another basket to hang. Don't run off."

As his mother went back up to the porch, Joy turned to him. "What time is it now, Daddy?"

"It's not time to go yet."

"Will you tell me as soon as it's time?"

"I will."

"Promise?"

"I promise. Do you believe me?"

She looked at him intently, then gave him a great big grin. "*Ja!* You always keep your promises."

"That's right, I do." No matter how painful it was to do so.

He shook off the thought. "Here comes your *gross-mammi* with another load. Let's help her hang up the clothes." He picked up Joy again.

"Someday I'm going to be big enough to do this by myself," she declared, struggling to place a clothespin on one end of the sheet his mother hung over the line.

Someday she would be, and he wouldn't be around to see it. The thought was a sobering one. He wanted to see her grow up. He wanted some part in who she became.

So, why couldn't he come back to visit? Now that he had faced his parents and gotten over that hump, was there really a reason he couldn't? Just because he couldn't live Amish didn't mean he had to cut himself off from Joy com-

pletely. Would his parents agree to his visits? He was sure his mother would.

Cheered by the idea, he started thinking about annual or semiannual trips home. He'd write and let his folks know he was coming so Wayne and Rhonda could avoid seeing him if that was how they wanted it. Perhaps in time, that rift could be mended, too.

He wanted to see Joy grow up. He wanted to be a part of her life, even if it was a small part. Until now, he'd only focused on the crisis in front of him. He'd been unable to look ahead. Now that he could, coming back for visits was a great idea.

He would tell Leah of his decision tonight. What would she think of it?

Trixie's barking alerted Leah and her friends Rebecca, Sarah and Joann to more visitors. Leah was surprised to see Caleb and Joy on her front porch when she opened the door. *"Gutenowed."*

Caleb looked ill at ease. "Good evening. I see by the buggies out here that you have company. I hope we're not imposing."

"I want to see Pickles. Can I, please?" Joy bounced beside him.

"Joy has been bugging me to let her visit the puppies again. My mother thought it would be all right if we came after you got home from school tonight."

Leah had mentioned tonight's baking frolic to Maggie and Rhonda at church. Maggie must have sent Caleb today because she knew Leah would have company. It eased the awkwardness of allowing Caleb into her home. Bless Maggie for being so considerate, but why hadn't she brought Joy?

Joy folded her hands together. "Please, can I see Pickles? I know she's missed me."

Grinning at the girl's excitement, Leah nodded. "I think she *has* been missing you. Come in."

Caleb, his shoulders hunched against the cold, said, "I can wait out here."

An outsider coming to visit a *maedel* who lived alone could be cause for talk. He was being protective of her reputation. That surprised her. It was odd how many things about Caleb Mast had surprised her in the past few days.

"You may come in. I'm sure you will remember most of my friends." She stood aside as he entered. He stopped only a few feet past the doorway as he took in the women seated around her kitchen table. Joy, when she realized there were more people in the room, became shy and hid behind her father.

Leah made the introductions. "Caleb, this is Joann Yoder, now Joann Weaver."

"I remember you from school."

"It is *goot* to see you again." Joann gave him a welcoming smile.

"Joann married Roman Weaver a few weeks ago."

"Congratulations. I heard about Roman's accident. I hope he makes a full recovery. Tell him I said hello."

"I will."

"Next is Sarah Beachy. She is married to Levi Beachy. I don't believe you have met Rebecca Troyer. She moved to Hope Springs a few years ago from Berlin. Her husband is Gideon Troyer, a cousin of Adam Troyer. This is Caleb Mast. He is Maggie's youngest."

He nodded to each of them in turn. "I'm sorry to crash your party."

He gently coaxed Joy forward. "This is my daughter, Joy. She is the one on a mission."

"'Cause I've been missing Pickles and she has been missing me," Joy declared.

Leah grinned at her friends. "Joy was here the day the puppies were born. She named the blond one."

"Pickles is a marvelous name," Joann said.

"Are you going to name the others?" Rebecca asked.

"Yup. They are Peanut Butter and Jelly."

Sarah was trying hard not to laugh. "Pickles, Peanut Butter and Jelly. I'd say those are some unusual but tasty names for puppies."

"If there had been a fourth one, you could have called it Church Spread," Joann added in all seriousness.

"What's that?" Joy asked, looking up at her dad.

Caleb smiled at her. "Church spread is peanut butter mixed with marshmallow cream."

"I had that Sunday. It was yummy." Joy closed her eyes, grinned big and rubbed her tummy, her shyness forgotten.

"My grandfather loved to eat his church spread with dill pickles. I don't have church spread, but I do have oatmeal raisin cookies. Would you like some?" Leah picked up a plate from the counter and held it out to Joy.

Joy glanced up at her father. He nodded. She quickly took two and rushed to the corner where Trixie lay with her pups.

Leah was left standing beside Caleb. She realized her friends were all watching her closely. She held the plate toward him and tried for a casual tone. Anything to hide the fact that her heart was racing as it always did when he was near. "We are getting ready for a cookie exchange at Rebecca's home on Friday. Would you like to sample some?"

"Oatmeal raisin is my favorite. How did you know?" He winked at her friends, as if she had made the cookies just for him.

Her smile turned chilly. "Your brother told me."

That took the grin off Caleb's face.

Instantly, she was sorry. No one at the table knew the full story about Leah's broken engagement. They only knew

that Wayne and Rhonda had had a hurry-up wedding. They certainly weren't the first young couple to have a babe arrive early. Only Sarah knew Leah had been serious about Wayne. It was never mentioned after the wedding took place. As upsetting as it was at the time, Leah realized now that she hadn't truly been in love with Wayne. She had been in love with the idea of marriage and starting a family of her own.

Would she have grown to love Wayne the way a wife should? She honestly didn't know.

She set the plate aside and joined Joy where she knelt by the puppies. "Would you like to hold Pickles?"

"Yes, please. Daddy said I wasn't to bug you about it. I was just to look at her."

"Then you have done very well to obey him." Leah lifted the pup from the blanket.

Joy took the puppy from Leah. "Has their daddy been here?"

"*Nee,* he has not come by again," Leah admitted.

"But it's almost Christmas. Pickles wants to see her daddy for Christmas."

Caleb said, "She has her mother and that's all she needs right now."

"No, she wants them both. See how unhappy she is. It's all right, Pickles." Joy hugged the puppy to console her.

Leah met Caleb's gaze. What was sad was the way Joy gave the puppy her own wants and needs.

Joann joined them. "May I hold a puppy?"

"Of course." Leah handed her friend the largest male.

"What do you think, Joy? Is this Peanut Butter, or is this Jelly?" Joann asked with a grin.

Joy gave the question careful consideration as she held Pickles next to her cheek. "I think that one is Peanut Butter. He has brown feet."

"Have you come home for a Christmas visit?" Rebecca asked Caleb.

"Something like that."

"Then you must bring Joy to our cookie exchange. I know she will enjoy it. There will be many children her age there. My husband would be delighted to meet you. He was out in the *Englisch* world for years before returning to us. He enjoys talking about cars and airplanes and all the things that he used to know."

Caleb shot a quick glance at Leah and then looked down at his boots. "Thank you for the invitation, but I'm not sure I can make it."

Sarah said, "We hope you can. We won't even require you to bring a pail of cookies, for I'm sure your mother will bring plenty. There will be more than enough for everyone. Leah, I think your last batch should be about done."

Leah glanced at the clock and hurried to her oven. The cookies were a little browner than she liked but thankfully not burned. She set the baking sheet on top of the stove and began removing the cookies. Caleb went to crouch beside Joy and admire the puppies. "They are getting bigger already."

Leah watched their interaction. It would be a good idea for Joy to interact with the other children on a fun occasion. Caleb would be reluctant to come if his brother and Rhonda were there. Maggie could bring the child, of course, but Leah found herself wishing that Caleb would come, too. The more he became involved in the community, the greater the chance was that he would change his mind and stay.

She transferred the last cookie and set the sheet aside to cool while she spooned more dough onto a second sheet. "Joann, have we heard who all is coming to the exchange?"

Joann's work at the paper left her privy to all the local goings-on. "I don't think there will be as many families there as last year. We're having it a week earlier, and it

turns out Esther Zook is hosting a quilting frolic for her niece on the same night."

Sarah moved to snitch a warm cookie from Leah's plate. "That means Grace and Henry Zook won't be there, but Levi and the twins are coming. What about Rhonda and Wayne?"

Leah resisted the urge to see if Caleb was listening. She bent and put a new tray of unbaked cookies in the oven. "Rhonda will go to the quilting bee. She mentioned that Wayne plans to visit with Bishop Zook about a church issue, so they won't be at the cookie exchange."

Joann replaced the puppy she was holding and returned to the table. "If our turnout is small, we can hold another one closer to Christmas."

Sarah said, "We should hold one when the twins are away visiting their grandmother. Then everyone can be assured that they will get home with cookies and not empty pails."

The women laughed. The twins, Moses and Atlee, were notorious pranksters.

Caleb stood and said, "Joy, it's time for the puppy to go back with her mother."

She replaced the puppy and gave Trixie a pat on the head. "Your baby likes me, but she needs you more. You are a good mommy."

"That's right," he said and took her hand.

Leah turned away from the stove with a dozen cookies wrapped in a blue-and-white-checkered napkin. She handed them to Joy. "A few for the road."

"Yum." Joy gleefully grabbed the offering.

"What do you say?" Caleb prompted.

"Thanks. I mean, *danki*."

Leah propped her hands on her hips. "Your *Deitsh* is getting better all the time."

"*Mammi* is helping me. Can I have a cookie now, *Daed?*"

"When we are in the buggy. Leah, will you walk us out?"

She hesitated and glanced at her friends, but they were busy looking through her recipe book for a new sugar cookie. She followed Caleb outside. He opened the door of the buggy for Joy and she hopped in. He said, "Now you can have one."

"Two?"

"One."

"Okay."

Leah grinned at Joy's dejected tone. Caleb turned to face her. "You don't have to do that."

"Do what?" she asked, even though she knew what he meant.

"You don't have to put yourself between my brother and me."

"I have no idea what you're talking about." She didn't want him thinking she had his interest at heart. Maybe she did, but she wasn't ready to admit it. Certainly not to him.

"You wanted me to know Wayne wasn't coming to the cookie exchange so that I could come. I don't want you to feel you have to take sides."

"I'm not."

"Then I'm glad you invited me. I'll be there." His voice grew warm and her pulse sped up.

She clenched her hands together to hide her growing jitters. "Joy will enjoy it."

"I will, too, if you are going to be there."

She stared at him in speechless shock.

He seemed to realize he'd gone too far. "Thanks again for being kind to Joy and including her. It helps knowing she will have a friend in you when I'm gone."

She gathered her scattered thoughts. "I wish you would reconsider that decision."

"Do you?"

He took a step closer. She didn't back away. His gaze softened. "Do you really want me to stay, Leah?"

Chapter Eight

Caleb's low, husky voice caused Leah's breath to catch in her throat. His nearness sent her pulse racing. Thick tension filled the air. His eyes held an emotion she didn't understand, but it pulled at her, making her want to move closer to him.

She had an overwhelming desire to lay her hand upon his cheek and study him until the riddle was solved. What would his skin feel like? She could imagine the rough texture of his whiskers, the heat that would warm her palm and spread through her body.

His lips were slightly parted as he gazed at her. When he kissed, would they be soft and inviting or hard and demanding? If she moved a step closer, would she discover the answer?

The boldness of her thoughts shocked her. She came to her senses and looked away to break the attraction growing between them. "I'm only thinking of Joy. She needs you to stay."

He moved back a pace. She sensed his disappointment. "Fair enough. Don't let your cookies burn."

He climbed into his father's buggy and gathered the reins. She took a step toward him, wanting him to stay longer, but she didn't know what to say.

Why did he confuse her this way? She was a level-headed person. She never flustered easily. So why was she flustered now?

He gave her a wry smile, as if he understood something she didn't. He clicked his tongue to set the horse in motion and drove away. She stood staring after him until the cold made her shiver.

She returned to the house to find her friends watching her with wide eyes. No one said anything. Finally, she asked, "What?"

"Caleb Mast has grown into a *gutguckich* fellow." Joann went back to studying the recipe book.

"A very good-looking man, indeed," Sarah agreed. "I liked him and his darling daughter."

"Do you think he means to stay among us?" Rebecca asked.

"I don't think so." Leah closed the door. She didn't feel right sharing Caleb's plans with her friends. They might not look so kindly upon him if they knew he intended to leave Joy with his parents and go back to his *Englisch* life.

Although why she should wish to protect him was a mystery to her. One she didn't care to examine too closely. Not with so many prying eyes watching her.

Rebecca smiled softly. "My Gideon did not know he wished to return to us until he came for my quilt auction."

Two years ago, the community had come together and held a quilt auction to raise money for a surgery that would restore Rebecca's sight. Gideon learned of his lost love's plight and returned to help. Leah was happy to stop talking about Caleb. "You mean Gideon didn't know he wanted to return until he saw *you* at the quilt auction."

Rebecca shrugged. "If I was the tool used to nudge Gideon back to God, I'm happy I was part of His plan. God moves in mysterious ways, you know. We all have a

part in His wondrous design though we may never know what that is."

Leah went to the stove, picked up her hot pad and opened the oven to check on her cookies. They needed another minute or two. She closed the door and put the hot pad aside. Was she part of some plan to help Caleb return to their community? It was hard to imagine a more unlikely scenario.

"Let's try this recipe for macaroons." Joann stabbed the page she was studying.

"Do we have all the ingredients it calls for?" Sarah leaned over to read it.

Joann looked at Rebecca. "I think I put a can of sweetened condensed milk in with the things I brought. Would you check and see if it's in that box on the counter?"

Rebecca came to stand beside Leah. She glanced into the box and said, "Yes, we have some."

Leah looked down at the oven. "They aren't ready yet."

"I guessed as much." Rebecca lowered her voice. "When I was blind, I spent a lot of time listening to people and reading what they thought in the tone of their voices. Now that God has seen fit to restore my sight, I spend a lot of time watching people."

"And?" Leah shifted uncomfortably.

"I see and hear something between Caleb Mast and you."

"You are mistaken." Leah opened the oven door again. The cookies still weren't ready. She closed the door with a bang.

"If you say so, I must accept that. Just remember that lying is a sin."

Leah yanked open the oven door and pulled out the cookie sheet anyway. "He's not one of us. He turned his back on his family and cast aside his faith. How could I have any feelings for a man like that except pity?"

The hot tray of cookies slipped sideways and she burned her fingers when she tried to save it. The pan clattered to the

floor, sending cookies tumbling across her kitchen. Dropping the sheet, she brought her stinging finger to her mouth.

Her friends rushed to help. Sarah and Joann cleaned up while Rebecca pulled Leah to the sink and ran cold water over her hand.

The pain was just punishment for her lie. It wasn't pity that made her heart race when Caleb was near.

What was wrong with her?

Caleb slapped the reins against the horse's rump to speed him up. No matter how fast Bobby trotted, he couldn't outrun Caleb's humiliation. He had made a fool of himself. There was no way around it.

Had he really expected Leah to say what he wanted to hear? That she wished he would stay for her.

Of all the women in the world, why did it have to be Leah Belier who turned him inside out? When he was close to her, his brain shut off and his emotions took over. She made him feel breathless, like a love-struck kid with his first crush.

Caring about her wasn't the problem. The consequences of pursuing her would be disastrous. For both of them. He had to get himself in hand. There couldn't be anything between them. She would never leave the Amish, and he couldn't stay.

Besides, Leah wasn't interested in him. Her interest was in Joy, not in Joy's wayward father.

"Do you want a cookie?" His daughter held the napkin toward him.

"Thanks." He selected one and took a bite. It was delicious. Of course Leah had to be a good cook, too. Good with kids, good with dogs, the only thing she wouldn't be good with was having Caleb Mast as a suitor.

He sat up straight. *Suitor* was a strong word. Was he re-

ally contemplating a relationship with her? He had to be out of his mind.

Joy sighed heavily. He glanced her way. "What's the matter, kiddo?"

"I'm tired. Why can't we drive places in the truck? We could be home by now."

"I thought you liked riding in the buggy. I'm using it out of respect for my parents. They believe that cars are worldly things. While we are staying with them, it's only polite to honor what they believe, even if I don't think that way myself."

"Are we going home to Texas soon? Mama might come see me for Christmas. She did last year."

How long would she hold on to that wish? Was it wrong for him to hope she would forget about Val and her life before coming to Hope Springs? "Your mama can come and see you here if she wants. I left word with Jake so she knows where we're staying."

"I don't think she can find me here. I don't think she likes me anymore."

"Your mother loves you and she always will." He hoped it wasn't a lie.

"Are Grandpa and Grandma really poor?"

That was an abrupt change of subject. "No. They just believe in living a simple life."

"Is Leah poor?"

"I don't know. Why?"

"Grandpa, Grandma and Leah don't have any Christmas decorations up. They don't have a tree or stockings hung. Nana said that sometimes poor people can't afford a Christmas tree."

How did he explain Amish reasoning to an eight-year-old who couldn't grasp complex ideas? "That's not the reason my parents and Leah don't have a tree. They believe

in celebrating the true meaning of Christmas, which has to do with the birth of Christ."

"The baby in the manger. I heard that story."

"Good. I'm glad." At least she'd had some exposure to the faith that was so important to the Amish community he hoped she could join. He should have explored the topic sooner.

"Do you think Santa Claus is going to be able to find me way out here?"

He hadn't given a single thought to how he should celebrate Christmas with her. Add another item to the list of things that made him a lousy parent. How would she react to the customs that were so very different from the ones she had grown up knowing?

"Joy, Santa Claus doesn't come to Amish homes."

"Why not? Are the Amish bad?"

"Of course not. Santa Claus doesn't come to Amish homes because he knows that the Amish don't need him to help celebrate the birth of Jesus."

"But I'm not Amish. I've been good. He's going to bring me presents, isn't he?" She sounded worried.

He quickly sought to reassure her. "There will be presents for you, Joy. They won't be fancy presents, and Santa won't bring them. Your grandpa, grandma and I will get them for you."

"How will you know what to get? Santa always knows and picks just the right presents, even if I don't tell him."

Was now the time to tell her that Santa was a myth? He decided that could wait. The poor kid was already being inundated with changes. Once she was older and came to understand the true meaning of Christmas, she would set aside her childish notions.

"We'll manage. Trust me. You're going to have a wonderful Christmas season full of all kinds of new things. Why, we are going to the cookie exchange in a few days.

We'll take a pail with us and fill it up with all kinds of yummy cookies. Doesn't that sound fun?"

"I guess, but what about our Christmas lights? Nana always put lights around the porch on our trailer."

"We won't have lights at the farm, but we'll go to town one of these nights to look at all the Christmas lights that are up there. If it snows enough, we'll go for a sleigh ride. Would you like that?"

"Is a sleigh ride fun? Is the sleigh pulled by reindeer?"

"It will be pulled by Bobby or maybe Grandpa's big draft horses if the snow gets real deep, but it's a lot of fun."

Sleigh rides were some of the best Christmas times in his memory. His family and friends piled under quilts as they raced over the snowy fields to have hot chocolate or hot spiced cider after caroling at neighbors' homes along the way. It didn't matter to them if the neighbors were Amish or *Englisch*. The season was for spreading joy to all.

He glanced sideways at his daughter. It wasn't like a trip to a fancy mall. Would she enjoy it? He hoped so.

She shook her head. "I'm not sure it can be Christmas without a Christmas tree, Daddy."

Maybe he was asking her to make too big of an adjustment. Just because he thought this might be the best life for her didn't mean she would feel the same way. "Let's try it this year and see how you like it."

"I'm gonna tell *Daadi* and *Mammi* that I want a tree. They will get one for me."

"I'm sorry, honey. They won't."

"But I want a Christmas tree! I want one. Pickles wants a tree, too. Mommy will have a tree at her place. I know she will. I want to go live with Mommy!" She threw her napkin on the floor and began kicking the front panel of the buggy.

The horse, startled by the sound, veered sideways, pulling the buggy into the wrong lane.

Caleb reined the horse back into line and made a grab for Joy. "Stop that!"

She screamed, and to Caleb's horror, she bolted out the door of the moving vehicle. He pulled to a stop as quickly as he could. "Joy! Joy, are you okay?" He looked back but couldn't see her.

A second later, he heard her crying. He dropped the reins, got out and ran to the back of the buggy. Joy was sitting at the bottom of a ditch, with blood smeared across her face. She had her hands cupped over her nose. He dropped to her side. "Hold still, kiddo. Where does it hurt?"

"I hit my nose," she mumbled through her fingers.

"Let me see." He pulled her hands aside and checked her over carefully. A bloody nose appeared to be the extent of the damage. Pulling a handkerchief from his hip pocket, he pressed it to her face. "You could have been hurt very badly. Never do that again."

Her tantrum forgotten, she struggled not to cry. "Are you mad at me?"

He pulled her into his arms. "*Liebschen,* you scared me out of ten years of my life, but I'm not mad. Please don't scare me like that again."

"You're squishing me."

He loosened his hold and looked at her face. "I'm sorry. Is that better?"

"Yes. What does *liebschen* mean?" Her voice was muffled beneath the cloth she held to her nose.

He chuckled as his fright faded, leaving him shaking like a leaf in the wind. The cold wet ground was seeping through his pants, but he didn't care. She was safe. "*Liebschen* means sweetheart."

"Am I your sweetheart?"

"Yes, you are. Let me see that nose." He took the cloth away. The bleeding had stopped.

"It still hurts."

"I'm not surprised. Joy, if you are upset about something, running away won't help. You need to talk to me about it or to Grandma or Grandpa. Do you understand that?"

"I guess."

Did she? Would she ever outgrow the habits that seemed so ingrained in her?

A car coming from the other direction stopped beside them. A gray-haired man rolled down his window. "Is everything okay?"

Caleb raised a hand and waved. "I think so."

The man put his flashers on and got out. "What happened?"

Caleb picked up Joy. "She jumped out of the buggy while it was moving and got a bloody nose for her trouble."

"Better let me have a look at her. I'm a doctor."

Caleb recognized Dr. Harold White. The elderly physician had managed a clinic in Hope Springs since before Caleb was born. He was well respected by the Amish who used his inexpensive services. "I remember you, Dr. White. I'm Caleb Mast. This is my daughter, Joy."

"Would you be Ike's youngest son? The one that moved away?"

"I am."

"I heard you were back in town."

It wasn't surprising. News traveled fast in the small community even though most residents didn't own phones.

Dr. White smiled at Joy as he carefully felt her head and neck and checked her over. "I put eight stitches in your daddy's foot when he was about your age. He cut himself on a piece of broken glass at a picnic."

Caleb stared at him in astonishment. "You have a very good memory."

"I never forget a patient. Well, young lady, you look just fine to me."

She shook her head. "I'm not fine. I have Down sindome."

Dr. White leaned back. "You mean Up syndrome, don't you? That's what I call it. Because the people with Up syndrome who I know are happy, not down and sad. My professional diagnosis is that you have Up syndrome."

She smiled at him. "*Ja,* I have Up sindome."

"Yes, you do." He looked at Caleb. "Keep an eye on her for behavior changes. If she develops a headache, bring her in to see me."

"I will."

Dr. White touched a finger to Joy's nose. "From now on, I want you to wait until the buggy isn't moving before you get out."

Caleb shifted her in his arms. "I think she has learned her lesson."

He carried her to the door and put her on the front seat. He turned and held out his hand to the doctor. "Thanks for stopping."

"Happy to do it. I was on my way home from seeing a patient who has a broken leg out this way."

"I didn't think doctors made house calls anymore."

"I do for some of my elderly or Amish patients if it's a hardship for them to come to me. I enjoy it. I'm glad you had a better outcome than the last time we met at an accident site."

Caleb felt his skin grow cold. "You were there?"

"I was. I've always been sorry that Rhonda's parents didn't allow her to have a repair on her face. With a little plastic surgery, her scars would have been much less noticeable."

"You know the Amish. It was God's will."

"Many Amish accept modern medical care, but I had to respect her father's decision even if I didn't like it. I never understood how you got out of that car without a scratch."

Caleb, uncomfortable with the way the conversation was going, climbed in the buggy with Joy. "It must have been God's will."

Dr. White didn't take the hint. He stood with his hand on the door, preventing Caleb from closing it. "God must have blessed you, indeed. I saw blood all over the door panel. I was sure you had been cut by the broken glass. You didn't have mud on your clothes, either. I remember thinking that was odd because, with the car upside down, you would have had to crawl out the window on your belly, and that field was very muddy that night."

"You must be mistaken. I recall being muddy."

"You know, in my mind, the investigating officer did a poor job that night."

"He sure hit me with a slew of tickets and a hefty fine. No driver's license, no insurance, no tags and reckless driving."

"And he came to collect your fine in person, didn't he?"

"He did." Caleb had been surprised when the young sheriff's officer with auburn hair and a superior attitude showed up at his home the next day. He demanded the fine be paid or Caleb was going to jail. Caleb's father handed over the money in silent disapproval. It took Caleb almost a year to pay him back.

Dr. White shook his head sadly. "Drake Colburn has engaged in some questionable behaviors. The Amish are easily taken advantage of because they don't report crimes. They pay their debts without question. I was glad when Nick Bradley, our current sheriff, fired Drake. Unfortunately, he's working for a neighboring county now. There are a lot of Amish in his new territory. I have encouraged several of my patients from the area to report his behavior, but I don't believe any of them have."

Dr. White took a step away from the buggy. "I'm keep-

ing you with my long-winded ways. Sorry. Take care, Joy, and come visit me sometime."

"Okay." She sat quietly on the seat beside Caleb, her outburst forgotten.

"It was good seeing you, Dr. White. Thanks again for stopping to help." Caleb closed the door, set the horse in motion and tried to relax.

Thinking about the night of the crash that injured Rhonda was something he didn't do. Ever. But hearing Dr. White's descriptions brought it all back as if it had happened yesterday.

The doctor had a good memory for details. Details that had been overlooked by everyone else. How strange that only an outsider had questioned Caleb's story.

Not that it mattered.

Caleb sighed heavily. He had lied to protect the brother he loved from shame. That lie, told for the best of reasons, had become a haunting, foul thing that hung between the brothers. Wayne, always the good son, hadn't been able to admit what he had done. He made Caleb promise never to reveal the truth.

Until Wayne released him from his promise to keep the events of that night a secret, the people who mattered, including Leah, would always believe the wild and reckless younger Mast brother had been behind the wheel the night Rhonda Belier was run down on the road near her home.

Caleb turned the buggy off the highway and into the lane that led to his father's house. Joy, exhausted from her ordeal, had fallen asleep on the seat beside him. If Leah knew the truth, would it change how she felt about him? Probably not, unless Rhonda admitted her lie, as well.

Why had she named him as the father of her child? What

did she hope to gain besides a reluctant husband? He had never understood. It was likely that he never would.

No matter how much he might enjoy Leah's company, their relationship was doomed.

Chapter Nine

On Thursday evening, at his mother's insistence, Caleb hitched her gray mare to her two-wheeled cart for the short drive to the Imhoff farm. He led the horse to the front gate and waited. His mother came down the walk with a large brown paper bag in her arms and handed it to him.

"What's this?" he asked.

"A rhubarb cake for the board to enjoy."

"Sounds delicious."

"Well-fed men are happy men."

"You'll get no argument from me on that score."

She climbed in the cart. After making certain that she was bundled against the cold with a thick lap robe, he hauled himself up beside her. "Are you sure you wouldn't rather take the buggy? It would be warmer."

"I enjoy being in the open. It's not that cold. You've grown soft in your years away."

He could see his breath in the air. It was cold. He glanced at the house. "Do you think *Daed* will be okay with Joy till we get back?"

"He managed with you and Wayne when you were that age."

"Yes, but Joy can be…difficult at times." He was think-

ing about the way she jumped out of the buggy yesterday. What if she took it into her head to run away again?

"They'll be fine. Stop fretting. I will drive if you don't care."

He handed her the reins. "Maybe I should stay home and let you go alone."

"*Nee*. As Joy's father, you should be the one to ask permission for her to attend school here."

He wasn't too sure about that. His presence could just as easily turn the board against his petition, especially since Wayne was a member. If they said no, he would go on to plan B. As soon as he figured out what that was.

It would take about fifteen minutes to reach the school. The Imhoff farm was two miles farther down the road. Caleb glanced at his mother as they turned out onto the highway. "What do you think they will do?"

"Eli Imhoff is the school-board president. He is a fair man. He will give our request due consideration."

"But he's not the only one on the board. What about the others?"

"Adrian Lapp is the secretary. He won't have a problem with Joy attending school at Walnut Valley. His adopted son, Kyle, was *Englisch* before coming to live among us."

"I hadn't thought of that." Was adoption plan B?

"Thought of what?"

"Letting you and *Daed* adopt Joy."

His mother scowled at him. "Would her mother agree to that?"

"If her parental rights are severed, she won't have a say."

"As much as I love Joy, I can't see taking her from her parents. The *Englisch* may have a law that allows it, but we do not."

So much for plan B. He didn't really care for the idea anyway. He wanted to be more a part of her life, not less.

He returned to the subject of the school-board meeting. "What position does Wayne hold?"

He sensed his mother's hesitation. "Wayne is the tax collector. Samuel Stutzman is the treasurer."

"Great. Samuel Stutzman never liked me. We might as well go home. This is a waste of time." Between Samuel and Wayne, Joy didn't stand a chance of getting into school.

"This is what you wish for your daughter. You can't give up so easily. Samuel is a contrary soul, to be sure. He rarely sees the bright side of things, and he is very set in his ways."

"You're not making me feel better."

"If something is his idea, then it is good idea. I have helped him see this was his idea."

Caleb looked at her in surprise. "When did you do that?"

"When you went to see Leah last evening, I went to visit Samuel and his wife. I took them a few jars of my rhubarb. Your father doesn't care for it and I know Samuel does. I simply told him how I wished Joy could come to know and love our ways as his children and grandchildren do. When I mentioned your plans to have Joy live with us, his wife said I should send her to an Amish school instead of sending her to the *Englisch* one."

"Okay, but how is that Samuel's idea?"

Maggie laughed. "Every husband whose wife has a *goot* idea soon believes it was his thought in the first place."

"I hope you're right."

Caleb pressed a hand to his stomach. He hadn't had butterflies like these in years. They weren't even butterflies, more like overgrown pigeons. As they approached the turn-off to Leah's home, he wondered if she was already gone. The monthly school-board meeting was when teachers received their salaries. He was surprised when his mother slowed her mare.

"What's wrong?"

"Nothing's wrong. Before we left the preaching service

last Sunday, I offered Leah a ride, since I knew we were going right by her place."

"And she accepted your offer? Did she know that I was going to be with you?"

"Of course. She thought it best for us to present a united front. The board may grant our request more readily if they know she is in favor of it."

He remained silent. His mother glanced his way. "Leah is an upright and caring woman. Joy is quite taken with her and speaks fondly of her."

Where was his mother going with this? "Leah has a dog with three puppies. Of course Joy is taken with her."

"It's more than the puppies. Joy truly likes her. Leah would make a wonderful mother, don't you think?"

"I'm sure she would. I hope you aren't thinking of matchmaking for us."

"Why would you say such a thing?" She pulled to a stop in front of Leah's gate.

He noticed she didn't deny the charge. Did she think a woman would keep him in Hope Springs? "I'm not going to stay, *Mamm.* Please don't get your hopes up."

She patted his knee. "A mother has many hopes for her children. You cannot change that with a few words."

Leah's front door opened, and she came out bundled up against the cold. She carried a large basket over one arm. He got down from the cart. "Let me help."

"Danki." She handed over her burden.

He set it behind the seat with his mother's cake and took Leah's elbow to help her up into the cart. When he got in after her, there was very little room for him to sit. She scooted over as far as she could. Easing into the space left, he had no choice but to put his arm along the back of the seat behind her. He practically had his arm around her. With his free hand, he arranged the lap robe over both of

them. His mother should have taken the buggy. This cart was too small for three adults.

"Is everyone cozy?" his mother asked with a bright smile. Before anyone answered, she set the horse into a brisk trot.

Leah had spent the past hour mentally preparing to spend a brief buggy ride to the meeting with Caleb in the same vehicle. She hadn't prepared for this.

Sandwiched between him and his mother, she was pressed against his side from shoulder to hip. She could feel the warmth of his body through her coat. She clutched the lap robe with both hands. "Maggie, was there something wrong with your buggy?"

"*Nee.* It's a fine evening, isn't it?"

"She likes to drive in the open," he muttered between clenched teeth.

"I do. It reminds me of the times Ike took me driving in his courting buggy. *Ach,* what a fine courtship we had. Your father was a romantic young man. He always brought some small gift that would make me smile."

"It sounds as if you were made for each other." Leah tried to edge away from Caleb, but it was useless. She had nowhere to go unless she moved onto Maggie's lap.

"I knew it from the first day I saw Ike at my cousin's wedding. What a handsome fellow he was. My parents didn't think much of him. He was too wild for their liking."

Caleb leaned forward to look at his mother. "*Daed* was a wild fellow?"

"*Ja.* So much like you when you were a boy, but I knew he would settle down and become a *goot* husband and father, and I was right."

Leah wondered what Maggie was trying to tell her. Was she hinting that Caleb would become a good husband and

father, too? It might happen, but not unless he changed a great deal.

He leaned close and whispered, "I'm sorry about this. Are you comfortable?"

"Well enough."

"It isn't much farther. I can walk home when the meeting is over."

"So can I."

"But you shouldn't have to. What's in the basket?"

"Cookies and brownies. Hungry men are cranky men. I thought I would sweeten them up before the meeting got started."

He laughed. The rumble from deep in his chest vibrated against her shoulder and arm. It sent a tingle of warmth through her. He had a nice laugh. Her discomfort forgotten, she gave him a quizzical look. "What's so funny?"

"You and my mother think alike."

"How so?"

Maggie chuckled. "I brought rhubarb cake."

Leah met Maggie's glance and they both laughed. The tension in the air eased and the rest of the ride passed quickly.

A large hand-painted sign depicting an anvil marked the lane of Eli Imhoff's farm. He was a blacksmith by trade and a horse breeder by choice.

The Imhoffs lived in a two-story white farmhouse with a smaller *dawdy haus,* a second home for elderly family members, connected to the main building by a covered porch with white railings and wide steps leading up to it. Three large birdhouses sat atop poles around the yard. The flowerbeds were empty now, but Leah knew they would be loaded with blooms from spring through fall. Nettie had a green thumb. There was already one buggy parked in front of the house.

Across a wide expanse of winter-brown grass stood a

large red barn and several outbuildings. In the corrals, a pair of enormous caramel-colored draft horses and a dozen Standardbred horses munched on hay bales. Eli was known far and wide as a breeder of fine trotters. Some of his horses, sold to *Englisch* trainers, had gone on to win major races.

Maggie pulled to a stop in front of the main house, and Caleb hopped down and offered his hand to Leah. She placed her fingers in his. Even through her gloves, she could feel his strength. He let go of her as soon as her feet touched the ground. Rounding the cart, he helped his mother down, too. Leah fetched her basket from the rear of the cart and followed Maggie to the front door. Once Caleb secured the horse, he came after them.

The door opened as they reached it. Nettie Imhoff stood aside. "Come in. Maggie, what were you thinking to travel in an open cart in this cold? I'll heat some bricks for you to use on the way home. No sense getting frozen toes."

"*Danki,* Nettie." Maggie stamped her feet. "It is a bit chilly out today. This is my son Caleb. I don't think the two of you have met."

Caleb nodded to her. "I don't believe we have."

"My son and I came to Hope Springs a few years ago from Pennsylvania after my husband passed away. Elam was hoping for a new start in a new place. We certainly got it. He married a fine girl, and I was blessed to find a man willing to put up with me and my set ways."

Eli walked into the room. "Don't let her fool you. She's the one who puts up with me and mine. Hello, Leah. I hope we can have a short meeting tonight. I've got a sick mare down at the barn."

She glanced at Caleb. "We do have a few things to talk about, but first, we brought some desserts."

"How nice. I'll get some plates." Nettie opened the cupboard door.

Eli grinned. "Dessert sounds wonderful. Don't marry

a pretty woman, Caleb. Marry a good cook. Looks fade, good cooking doesn't."

Nettie stopped and turned around with a plate in her hand. "Are you saying my looks are gone?"

Eli realized his mistake. *"Nee,* you're a fine-looking woman, Nettie, and a *wunderbaar* cook. I'm a doubly blessed man."

She shook the plate at him. "You are, and don't forget it."

The outside door opened and a tall Amish man with a thick reddish-brown beard entered the kitchen. He carried a black notebook. His wide smile included everyone in the room. *"Gutenowed."*

Eli said, "Good evening, Adrian. You've come just in the nick of time."

Adrian hung his black hat on a peg beside the door and then scanned the room. His eyes widened when they settled on Caleb. "Caleb Mast, is that you? It's been many a year since I laid eyes on you. How has the *Englisch* world been treating you?"

"Well enough, Adrian. Good to see you again." Caleb was heartened by the reception he was receiving. Maybe Wayne hadn't turned everyone against him.

The door opened again and Samuel Stutzman came in. He hung his hat beside Adrian's. He stared at Caleb without greeting him, and then he nodded to all the others. "Blessings be upon this house."

Acceptance by everyone was too much to hope for.

Eli laid a hand on Samuel's shoulder. "Why don't we get out of the kitchen and let our women have their space? Come into the living room and have a seat."

Caleb glanced at his mother and Leah. They both gave him an encouraging nod. He left his moral support in the kitchen and followed Eli. Chairs had been arranged on both sides of the living room. They must be expecting a fair number of parents to attend.

Eli settled in a winged-back chair near the fireplace. "So, what brings you to our school-board meeting?"

Apparently, Eli didn't believe in beating around the bush. Adrian and Samuel took a seat on the couch but didn't say anything. Adrian opened his notebook and pulled a pen from his pocket.

Caleb cleared his throat. "I have a daughter who is eight years old. Her name is Joy. She has Down syndrome."

"I met her at the church service. My daughter Anna introduced us. You are blessed to have such a special child."

Caleb drew a deep breath. "In the *Englisch* world, a child such as Joy is not always treated as a blessing."

Eli nodded. "I understand that this is so. It is a sad thing when people cannot see the beauty in all God's creations."

"Joy's life has not always been happy. It is my wish that she grow up here."

Eli laced his fingers together over the slight paunch of his belly. "Both you and your daughter will be welcome if you are accepted back into our faith. You should speak with Bishop Zook. He can guide you in this matter much better than I."

"That's the thing. I don't wish to live Amish. While I believe it is the best thing for my daughter, it is not the life for me."

A troubled frown marred Eli's jovial face. He shared a speaking glance with Adrian and Samuel, and then said, "Such an arrangement will be very confusing for your child. Our ways are not easy. It is the solemn duty of a parent to teach by example. If you do not live as we do, how can you expect your daughter to learn, respect and adhere to our ways?"

"Joy will live with my parents, not with me. I'm here tonight to ask that she be allowed to attend Walnut Valley School even though I am no longer Amish." Caleb fell silent as Leah came in with a plate in each hand.

"Eli, would you like a brownie, rhubarb cake or both?"

"Cake will be fine." He accepted the plate she handed him. "Did you know about this?"

She flashed a scowl at Caleb. He should have waited until after the cake to make his request. "I learned of Caleb's plan last week."

Eli raised an eyebrow at her admission. "Perhaps it would have been better to discuss it with me before now."

"I'm sorry. I thought it would be better to present the idea to the entire board."

"I see. What do you think of allowing an *Englisch* child to attend your school?" Eli took a bite of his cake.

She handed a plate to Adrian. "Joy will be a wonderful addition to my classroom, just as Kyle has been."

Lifting his fork, Eli pointed at her. "Who will you go to if there are problems with the girl?"

"Caleb, of course. Also Maggie and Ike, since she will live with them."

Adrian spoke up. "Where will you live, Caleb?"

Caleb hesitated. This was going to be the tricky part. "Texas for now, but I plan to spend a year in Brazil. I work on off-shore oil rigs. My parents will make all decisions about Joy while I'm away."

Samuel said, "I think the child should be allowed to attend school. I said as much to Maggie just the other day. Maggie and Ike have always supported our school. So does Wayne. I see little reason why we should deny this request."

"What does Joy's mother think of this arrangement?" Adrian asked.

"She isn't in the picture. She left Joy in my care and took off. I don't know where she is."

Eli clearly wasn't pleased with the information. "And now you will leave Joy in the care of your parents and take off."

"No one can do a better job of raising Joy than my par-

ents. I wish I could be the one to raise her, but my job takes me away for long periods of time."

Caleb heard the outside door open again. A small group of parents entered. Greetings and chatter filled the kitchen. Wayne entered the room and stopped short at the sight of Caleb. His face grew red with agitation and he looked to Eli. "I can have no part of this meeting with this man here."

Turning on his heels, he started to leave, but Caleb shot to his feet. "Don't go. I've finished all I came to say. Please continue your meeting. Eli, thank you for hearing me."

Caleb walked into the kitchen, where Rhonda stood beside his mother. She averted her face. He spoke to his mother. "I'll walk home. See you there."

He went out the door and stopped at the gate as he waited for the cold air to cool his temper. If his brother couldn't manage a single civil conversation, what hope was there for them?

"Caleb?"

He turned at the sound of Leah's voice. "I'm fine. Go back in."

She came down the steps and stood beside him. "I will plead Joy's case to them."

Did she have any idea how much her kindness meant to him? He gave a slight nod. "I know. Thanks. I wish… Never mind what I wish. Do what you can. If they say no, I'll enroll Joy in the public school in town. They might change their minds in a year or two with me out of the picture."

Her chin came up. "I will see that they do."

Her bravado made him smile. "Joy couldn't have a better champion. Good night, Leah Belier."

"*Guten nacht,* Caleb Mast. Take care."

The following afternoon, Leah had only been home from the cookie exchange for a few minutes when she heard a buggy come into the yard. Eli and Nettie Imhoff got out of

it. The school-board meeting had adjourned without making a decision about Joy. They had planned to meet again at Wayne's home this afternoon. Had they come to a decision?

Leah had been disappointed, but not surprised, when Maggie and Joy came to the cookie exchange without Caleb. Joy had had a good time playing with Anna and Emmy Chupp. It gave Leah hope that she would assimilate into the community and form lasting bonds.

Leah invited Eli and Nettie in and waited impatiently for them to get settled. She was eager to learn the verdict, but she couldn't neglect her duties as the woman of the house. When they were situated in her living room with cups of steaming coffee in their hands, she took a seat in her rocker and waited for Eli to speak.

He took a sip of his coffee. Nettie, brimming with excitement, said, "They have decided that Joy can attend our school."

Leah breathed a prayer of thanks. Eli gave his wife a sour look. She sat back with a grin on her face, not the least bit intimidated, and blew on her coffee to cool it.

He said, "That was our decision. Joy Perry may attend Walnut Valley School. Although her father does not follow our ways, the majority of us believe it is good that he wishes his daughter to do so. We wanted you to be the first to know, since the responsibility for her education will fall directly on you. If you have any concerns that you felt you could not express in front of Maggie and Caleb, I would hear them now and hold them in confidence."

Did she have reservations? No. Teaching was the path God had chosen for her. Providing an education for Joy was what she was meant to do. "I'm delighted with the decision. I'm sure that Maggie and Ike will provide all the support I need if there are problems. When can she start?"

"On Monday if you and her father agree."

It was Friday evening. "That won't give Joy's family

much time to purchase the supplies she will need for the rest of the school year. I do keep a stash of extra supplies for emergencies here at home."

"A sound idea after what happened last summer," Nettie said sadly.

Last summer an arsonist had set fire to the school. By the grace of God, the building had survived with only moderate damage, but all the children's books and records had been destroyed. Although it was an event that was unlikely to be repeated, for the arsonist had been arrested, Leah now made sure she kept only part of her records and supplies there.

Eli said, "I spoke privately with Caleb before the board met again. He has agreed to pay his fair share to the school district just as any parent would. Although he will not live in the area, he has expressed his intention to return several times a year to help with the physical upkeep of the school. I saw that as more than fair."

"He intends to return?"

Eli nodded. "That's what he told me."

It was the first Leah had heard of such a plan. She had heard him express only his intention to leave and allow his daughter to live an Amish life with his parents. When had he had this change of heart? Perhaps his attachment to Joy was growing.

When the couple had finished their coffee, Leah took their cups and carried them into the kitchen. Eli and Nettie followed her, stopping beside Trixie's box to admire the puppies. Nettie picked up one of the boys. "Elam was just saying the other day that he'll soon need a dog to help control his flock."

"Trixie is very good at gathering in the geese and ducks. I'm sure her puppies will be, too."

Nettie laughed. "He has neither geese nor ducks. What

he and Katie need help with is their gaggle of children. They have three now, and I reckon that's not the end of it."

"*Nee,* not the way he smiles when he looks at her," Eli said with a grin.

Nettie laid a hand on his arm. "He smiles at her the way you smile at me."

The widow and widower had wed two years ago, and it was clear they were every bit as much in love as the youngsters in the family. Leah knew a moment of envy. Why wasn't there someone for her to love?

Nettie reached for her coat. "We are on our way to see Maggie and Ike and let them know the school board's decision. Would you like to come with us?"

There was no real reason for her to go, but Leah pulled her own coat off the hook, excited at the idea of seeing Caleb again. And Joy. "I would. In case Maggie or Ike has questions for me. And I can deliver the supplies to Joy. It will only take me a minute to get together what she will need."

Twenty minutes later, they pulled up in front of the Mast farmhouse. Maggie opened the door and invited them in. Ike came in from the living room. Eli said, "I would speak with you about the education of your granddaughter. Is her father about?"

"He and Joy have gone down to the barn to feed the horses. I will get him." Ike reached for his hat.

Leah said, "I'll go."

"Very well."

Outside, Leah hurried across to the old red barn. The wind was cold as it blew down from the north, pushing a flurry of snow with it. Inside the relative comfort of the barn, she pushed her bonnet back and adjusted her *kapp*. She located Caleb by the sound of his voice coming from the hayloft. He was talking softly to someone, most likely to Joy.

Leah pressed a hand to her heart to still the sudden rush of pleasure that raced through her at the sound of his voice. In spite of her misgivings, she had come to care a great deal about him. Much more than was wise. How could she have allowed this to happen?

Recognizing the attraction for what it was, she knew the best thing for her was to turn and walk away.

Chapter Ten

Leah's common sense told her to call out to Caleb and Joy and then return to the house. She opened her mouth but heard the sound of Joy's giggle and remained silent. Maybe she was being foolish, but she adored spending time with Joy. Whatever they were doing sounded like fun. She would guard her heart against becoming more involved with Caleb now that she understood what was happening.

She climbed the ladder to the haymow and followed the sound of Joy's giggles. She found father and daughter lying in a pile of hay, staring at the rafters. Joy spied her first. She held a finger to her lips. "Shh."

Caleb rose on one elbow. A piece of straw dangled from his lips. He whispered, "We're watching a barn owl."

Leah looked up. "Truly? They're an endangered species in this state. Where is it?"

"On the rafter near the center of the barn, just slightly to the left. It looks as if he's been roosting here for a while."

"I still don't see him."

Joy said, "If you lie down, you can see him better and your neck won't get tired. What's *endangered*?"

Leah stepped across the hay and sat down beside Joy. She wrapped her arms around her knees, conscious of the fact that Caleb was stretched out on the other side of his

daughter. The classroom wasn't the only place to share knowledge. Times like this were perfect to teach children about nature and the gifts of God. "Endangered means there aren't very many of them anymore. Barn owls love to live in barns and old silos, but many of those have been torn down to make way for houses and towns, so the barn owls don't have places to live anymore."

"That's sad."

"It is. Did you know they are sometimes called a flying mousetrap because they eat so many mice? They truly are a farmer's friend. I still don't see him."

Caleb removed the piece of straw he had in his mouth. "Give your eyes time to adjust to the dark. I assume you are here because you heard from the school board."

Leah lay back beside Joy and closed her eyes. "I did. Eli and Nettie brought me over. They are inside speaking with your parents."

"Let me guess. Wayne got them to vote against me."

She opened her eyes and turned in his direction. The worried frown on his face put a crease between his brows. She was happy to give him the good news. "*Nee,* he was overruled by the others. She can start on Monday."

Caleb sat up. "Are you serious?"

"I am."

Joy pointed overhead. "He's looking at us. He can turn his head all the way around. Cool."

Leah leaned close to follow Joy's finger. "I see him now. His face is so pretty and white. Doesn't he have huge eyes? They help him see at night. Maybe he thinks we are giant mice here in the straw."

"That's silly. We don't have big ears, and we don't have tails."

"Very true. Joy, how would you like to come to school on Monday?" Leah asked.

"I don't know. Would I have to go alone?"

"There are twenty-seven other children in my school, so you can't possibly be alone."

Caleb stretched out in the hay once more. "You wouldn't have to walk to school alone, if that's what is worrying you. I will go with you and spend the day. How would that be?"

"I guess that would be okay. Are the other kids going to think I'm stupid?"

"Nee," Leah answered quickly. "They are going to see what a very special person you are. You can be a big help to me at school, you know."

"How?"

"Just by speaking English. It helps the younger children learn the language when they hear it spoken. Anna Imhoff is very excited that you will be in our school."

"I like Anna. She's really nice to me. Oh, look. The owl is gone. Where did he go?"

Caleb sat up and tickled her chin with a piece of straw. "He went out to hunt for his supper. He doesn't have a *grossmammi* to cook for him. He has to go find food himself. Shall we go in and see what *Mammi* has cooked for us?"

"I want to stay out here in case he comes back." She folded her arms over her chest.

"Nope. No arguments. Leah and I are going inside. If you stay out here, you will make your grandmother worry about you. She'll be mad at us for leaving you out here alone. Do you want to get us in trouble?"

She mulled over the idea and shook her head. "No."

Each time Leah saw Caleb with Joy, she was amazed at the difference in him. The frantic, frazzled man she first met outside the grocery store had become a caring and compassionate parent. He was making an effort and making progress at becoming a father. She could see the love for his child growing stronger every day, and it pleased her.

He helped Joy to her feet and began brushing away the

bits of straw stuck to her coat and bonnet. "You had better brush me off, too. I don't want to carry all of this into Grandma's clean house."

Joy energetically brushed the back of his pants and as high as she could reach on his back. "I can't get it all. Leah, can you help me?"

Leah rose to her feet and shook out her skirt. Caleb held his arms out to his sides. She moved close and set to work picking the straw off his coat, ignoring the way her insides fluttered at his nearness. She smoothed away the loose bits from across his shoulders. Even through the thick material of the coat, she could feel the firmness of his muscles. She could tell he was used to hard physical work. Slowly, she brushed down each arm. Finally, all that was left was a few pieces of straw in his hair.

Without thinking, she slid her fingers up the nape of his neck. His hair was short but thick. It felt like soft fur beneath her fingers. When she realized what she was doing, she stepped away quickly. "Clean as a whistle."

He cleared his throat. "Thanks. We should go."

"*Ja.* Eli and Nettie are probably wondering what happened to me." She started toward the ladder, but he stopped her by grasping her arm.

"They will think you've been rolling in the hay. Hold still a second."

Standing behind her, he gently brushed at her back. He kept one hand on her shoulder to steady her. In the space of a few seconds, it went from a friendly gesture to an intimate experience. She could feel his breath on the back of her neck. His hands stopped moving and rested on her shoulders. Her own breathing became ragged. If she turned around, would he kiss her?

"Come on, guys. I'm getting hungry."

Embarrassment sent a wave of heat to Leah's face. She'd completely forgotten about Joy. "We're coming."

* * *

Caleb watched as Leah quickly followed Joy down the ladder. Once again, he had let his growing desire override his common sense. Yet Leah hadn't rejected him outright. She'd tolerated his touch, but what did that mean, exactly?

She kept her attention on Joy and held her hand as they crossed the yard. "I've brought your books and some supplies. Pencils, crayons, paper and such. You have all you need to begin school."

She stopped at the buggy and drew a bag from the backseat. She handed it to Joy. "Don't forget to bring it to school on Monday."

"I won't." Joy gazed up at her with admiration shining in her eyes. Caleb knew exactly how she felt. Leah always seemed to know what Joy needed.

Inside the house, Nettie and Maggie were busy at the stove. Maggie said over her shoulder, "Ike and Nettie are staying for supper. I hope that is okay with you."

Leah smiled, but it was stiff. She cast a sidelong glance his way and then quickly looked at his mother. "What can I do to help?"

"You and Joy may set the table."

The meal was one of the longest that Caleb had ever endured. Leah sat across from him and spent the entire time trying not to look at him. It was a relief when everyone finished. The men went into the other room while the women began to clean up.

Eli moved a small round table and positioned it between two chairs. "How about a game of checkers?"

Ike pointed to Caleb. "Better warm up with the boy before you take me on."

Eli snorted. "It will be a rare day that I can't best you, but take a seat, Caleb, and give your father a short reprieve. Will you be black or red?"

"Red." Caleb sat down and put his pieces on the board,

but his mind wasn't on the game. It was on Leah. What was she thinking? Did she find his touch repulsive? If not, where did they go from here?

The short answer was nowhere.

Eli beat him soundly in record time. Caleb looked to his father. "*Daed,* why don't you have a go at him? You always were a better player than I was."

Ike rose from his chair. "Are you ready to take your beating, Eli?"

"Ha! You can try."

Caleb watch them set up a new game and then wandered to the doorway that led to the kitchen.

Joy sat quietly at the table with her chin propped on her hands. She had been quiet throughout the meal. Was she feeling okay?

"What's the matter, Joy? Do you have a headache?" he asked. It was something Dr. White had told him to watch for.

"No."

Maggie pressed a hand to her forehead. "You aren't warm. Do you feel sick?"

"*Mammi,* your house isn't very Christmassy."

She still wanted a Christmas tree. Caleb wondered how his mother would handle the request.

Maggie looked around the room. "I reckon you're right. Do you want to help me fancy it up?"

Joy brightened. "Sure. Can we put up a Christmas tree?"

"*Nee,* child, for that is a worldly thing. It is not permitted. I know something we can do. I've been getting Christmas cards from my friends and family for the past few weeks. I keep them in a box in my bedroom. Wait a moment and I will get it."

She returned shortly and set a shoe box on the table. "Let's put them up so everyone can enjoy them. Leah,

would you get me a ball of yarn from my knitting basket by the fireplace?"

"Of course." While Nettie, Maggie and Joy began sorting through the cards, Leah approached Caleb. He was blocking the doorway. She paused in front of him but kept her gaze on the floor. Softly he said, "I didn't mention how nice you look tonight."

Color bloomed in her cheeks. She smoothed the front of her dark green dress with its matching apron. "This is only one of my school dresses. It's not new. In fact, it's a little stained and worn."

"Actually, I hadn't noticed your dress."

Her eyes flashed up and locked with his. He didn't flinch from her gaze. He wanted her to know that he saw her, and he liked what he saw. He stepped aside. She rushed past him. Quickly, she came back with a ball of yarn, but she avoided looking at him. Caleb followed her into the kitchen and took a seat across from his daughter at the table.

"What do we do now?" Joy asked.

Maggie glanced around her kitchen. "I reckon we have to decide where we want to hang our cards. Then we will put up some yarn and hang the cards on it. Where do you think they should go?"

Joy looked around. "I'm not sure."

"You used to hang them across the windows when I was little." Caleb began reading some of the cards. A few of them were store-bought cards, mostly from the English neighbors and shopkeepers in the town. The others, from family and Amish friends, were homemade and decorated by hand.

"All right, we'll start with the windows." His mother opened one of the kitchen drawers and pulled out some thumbtacks.

With Nettie's help, she stretched three strands of yarn across the large windows that looked out onto the front

porch and then stood back with her hands on her hips. "Do those look straight?"

"They look fine," Caleb said. "Joy, why don't you pick out the ones you want to hang up?"

"Okay." She began sorting through the box. "I like this one, and this one." She handed them to Leah, who was seated beside her. Leah took them to the window.

"Daddy, you hang up these." She handed him a small bundle.

Caleb worked silently beside Leah until Nettie began to hum a Christmas song. Leah started humming, too. Soon Caleb began to sing the well-known hymn, "O Little Town of Bethlehem," and Leah, Maggie and Nettie all joined in.

Still singing, he went back to the table and picked up Joy. He carried her to the window so that she could hang the rest of the cards she had chosen.

When the song was finished, Joy clapped her hands. "Now it looks more like Christmas."

Eli and Ike came to the doorway. Ike said, "I reckon I could bring in a little greenery for the mantel tomorrow."

Maggie smiled at him. "*Ach,* that would be *wunderbaar.* I love the way the pine branches make the house smell."

Caleb reached for his coat. "No reason to wait until tomorrow. I can go cut a few now."

"But it's dark outside already," his mother said.

"I've got a flashlight."

Maggie turned to Ike. "Go with him and hold the light."

"These old bones don't want to go back out in the cold."

Caleb saw his chance. "Leah, would you come hold the flashlight for me?"

"That's a good idea. Thank you, Leah." His mother smiled at them both.

His father came to the table. "Joy, would you like to make some Christmas cards to send to your friends back in Texas?"

"I don't know how."

Ike sat down at the head of the table. "I will help you. Mama, do we have some colored paper?"

"We do. I have cutouts of flowers and birds and butterflies. I collect them all year for just this reason. I have glue, too."

"Leah brought me colors. Can I use them?"

"*Ja.* We will make some lovely cards to send to your friends." Maggie left the room and returned with another, larger box.

The adults all took a seat at the table to join in on the card making. Nettie began another song and soon everyone was singing along.

Caleb put on his coat and held Leah's for her. She slipped into it and quickly stepped away. He took a flashlight from the cabinet and held it out to her as he opened the door. She took the light and walked out ahead of him.

The clouds had moved on and a clear, star-filled sky arched overhead. The moon was a slim crescent rising in the east.

She turned the flashlight onto his face, making him squint against the brightness. "What did you want to talk to me about?"

He turned his face away. "I don't know what you mean."

"I assumed you wished to speak to me privately, since you asked me to accompany you outside."

"Can you shine that light somewhere else?"

"Sorry." She aimed it at the ground.

"Thank you. I didn't have anything special I needed to tell you. I just wanted your company. I'll get the saw from the shed. Mind if I use your light?"

"Not at all." She sounded confused. He didn't blame her.

His ulterior motive was to spend time alone with her, but he did have questions about Joy. Perhaps it was better to get on a safe subject.

"I know you've had a chance to read Joy's records. Do you think she is ready for the second grade?"

"I don't think so. Her grandmother kept very poor records. I don't believe she put a lot of effort into educating Joy. I could be wrong. I can evaluate her and make a better judgment in a few days."

"I don't want her to feel bad about not keeping up with the kids her age."

"I think I will be able to manage that part of it. As long as she feels included and comfortable, I don't think she'll realize that she is behind others her age. This will be her first public school. She won't have anything to gauge it against."

"She ran away from the private school I enrolled her in."

Leah shrugged. "She may do the same at Walnut Valley. We won't know until we give it a try."

He collected the saw from inside the shed, and by unspoken consent, they began walking into the woods along the path that led to the school. "I'm sure you'll make her feel comfortable. You have that effect on people. Will my being at the school make you uncomfortable?"

"*Nee,* parents visit our classroom often."

"I'm not exactly your run-of-the-mill Amish parent."

She tipped her head slightly to study him. "You are getting there. I see a little pine tree that looks eager to donate some branches to help celebrate our Lord's birth." She pointed the flashlight to the side of the trail.

Caleb walked up to the small fir tree. It was only about six feet tall and shaped like a perfect Christmas tree. "It's a shame I can't take the whole thing back for Joy. She wants a Christmas tree so badly. I didn't realize how hard it would be for her to give up all the English trappings of the season."

"Are they hard for you to give up?"

"Me? I never bothered with a Christmas tree. My condo was too small. Christmas was just another day for me."

"Then it is a good thing that Joy has come into your life to make Christmas meaningful again."

He smiled softly as he remembered meeting his daughter for the first time. "She told me her nana used to say she was her special Christmas Joy because she was born on Christmas Day. I think Joy believes the holiday decorations are there to celebrate her birthday.

"Mom intends to make her a special birthday cake and have a small family celebration on Christmas night. You're invited to come."

Leah grinned. "I will. We want her to know her birthday is important to us, too."

He trimmed a few of the lower, longer branches to take back to the house. Hopefully it would be enough to give Joy the sense of Christmas that she craved.

Leah walked all around the small tree. "I see no reason why Joy can't have her Christmas tree. It wouldn't be right to cut it down and bring it into the house. That would be worldly. But to put a few homemade decorations on this little tree out here for just the two of you would be an acceptable thing.

"We can make decorations that will look pretty and feed the birds, as well. Stale popcorn strands with dried berries. Perhaps some orange slices or apple slices smeared with peanut butter and coated with birdseeds. No one would object to such a useful tree."

It was the perfect solution. Why hadn't he thought of it? He looked at her in amazement. "How do you do it?"

"How do I do what?"

He stepped closer and spoke softly. "How do you see what others need and find a way to give it?"

She gazed at his face. He could see the starlight reflected in her eyes. Her white *kapp* outlined her face with a circle of brightness in the dark.

"I don't do anything special."

"Yes, you do. You do something special for my child every time you see her. You calm her, you teach her, you encourage her and you bring her joy. You have a very special gift."

She looked away. Was she uncomfortable with his praise? "The Lord gives us what we need to follow the path He has chosen for us. Teaching is my calling. Any gifts I possess are given by Him."

Caleb placed a finger beneath her chin and lifted her face until she was looking at him. "Then for the first time in a long time, I give thanks to Him for what He has brought into my life. You."

Caleb ached to kiss her. He wanted it more than he wanted his next breath. They were cocooned by the night. The scent of fresh-cut pine filled the air. He leaned toward her slowly, waiting to see if she would reject him or welcome him.

He didn't get the chance to find out. His mother's voice broke the connection between them as she called their names.

Leah stepped back quickly. "We must return to the house."

"I'd rather stay out here with you."

She turned and raced away, leaving him standing alone in the darkness.

He curled his cold fingers deep in his pockets. Something told him that Leah was the woman he'd been waiting his whole life to find. Did she feel the same? He longed to know.

Yet even if she did, how could they make a life together?

Chapter Eleven

"I'm so excited. Were you excited on your first day of school, Daddy?"

Joy swung her red-and-white lunchbox from one hand as she walked beside Caleb on Monday morning. She wasn't exactly walking, more like bouncing. She wore a simple blue dress and a black *kapp* beneath her black coat and bonnet. She had gray snow pants on under her dress to keep her legs warm on the walk to school. The pants would come off once she was at school and would be put back on for recess outside and the walk home.

"I was about as excited as you are."

Almost as excited as he was now at the thought of seeing Leah again. Their moments together on Friday night replayed in his mind. If his mother hadn't called to them, he would have kissed Leah.

He was almost sure she would've let him.

He intended to test his theory at the first opportunity. Better to know than to spend another sleepless night wondering. She had been on his mind constantly even though he knew nothing could come of their relationship. He wasn't going to stay in Hope Springs and Leah would never leave the Amish. Or would she? Was it wrong to hope she might consider a life outside the Amish?

A small voice at the back of his mind reminded him there was another choice. He could stay and resume his Amish life.

Was that really a possibility? Two weeks ago he would have said no. Now the idea didn't seem so farfetched. Wasn't he happier now than he'd ever been in the English world?

"I know my ABCs, Daddy. Do you want to hear them?" Joy looked at him hopefully.

"Sure."

"A. B. C." She smiled brightly.

"So far so good. Can you say the rest of them?" He scanned the woods, hoping to see a glimpse of Leah. She was probably already at the school.

"A. B. C. That's the ABCs."

"What if I asked you to say the alphabet? Could you do that?"

Her happiness faded. "I don't think so."

"I happen to know the entire alphabet. I'll help you learn it."

"For real?"

"For real."

"What will I do in school?"

"Oh, lots of things. Leah is going to help you learn to read and write and to do your sums. You're going to learn history and geography. You'll learn things like how to drive a buggy and share the road with cars."

"It's gonna be so fun."

"I hope so," Leah said. She was sitting on a fallen log off to the side of the trail. In her dark coat and bonnet, she had blended into the pines behind her. If she hadn't spoken, he might've walked past her. She was waiting for them.

"Good morning. I was afraid we had missed you." A surge of pleasure filled him when he saw her shy smile.

She rose to her feet and joined them. "I didn't want to

miss walking to school with Joy on her very first day at Walnut Valley."

"Am I really going to learn to drive a buggy?" Joy asked.

"Not today, but you will learn many practical things at school."

"How is Pickles? Has her daddy come to see her?"

"No, Duncan hasn't been over."

"He's not a very nice daddy," Joy declared.

"I'm sure he's just been busy taking care of all Woolly Joe's sheep."

"I miss Pickles."

Leah glanced at Caleb. "You must ask your father to bring you over to see her again. She's becoming a little butterball. She is bigger than both her brothers."

Joy said, "I wish I had a brother. Dad, can I have a brother one of these days?"

The light mood of the morning vanished. Caleb knew exactly what Leah was thinking. She was thinking that David was Joy's half brother. What would it take to convince her it wasn't true?

He said, "I think you should stick to wishing for a dog."

Joy continued talking nonstop, but the adults walked in silence. When they finally reached the school building, Leah set about her work and got the fire going. Caleb brought in two buckets full of coal and then took a broom to clear the snow from the front steps.

Joy spent the time exploring the room and chatting away. Leah showed Joy her desk in the first row and helped her unpack her supplies and stow them. When it was warm enough, Leah had her put her coat and bonnet in the cloak room. Together, they made a sign with Joy's name on it and hung it over the hook so that she would be able to find her things later.

The other students began arriving in family groups thirty minutes later. They were noisy as they filed in, call-

ing greetings to each other and to Leah. Joy, overcome with
shyness, moved to stand beside Caleb.

Some of the children brought out potatoes wrapped in
aluminum foil and placed them on a ledge to roast inside
the furnace door. Two brothers brought out soup in a glass
jar and set it on top of the stove. Leah filled a kettle with
water and placed it on top of the stove, as well, to provide
moisture in the air.

One excited little girl with blond pigtails ran up to Leah.
"*Teetshah, Mamm* has a *nei boppli.*"

"That's wonderful, Ammia, but you must remember to
speak English when you are at school."

Ammia concentrated a moment and then said, "Teacher,
my mama has a new *boppli.*"

"A new baby."

"*Ja,* and it's a girl. Her name is Mary. I have a *shvesh-
tah.*"

"You have a sister. I'm so glad for your family. Your
mother and father must be very happy. Now, you should
take your seat. We have a lot to do today."

Caleb moved to a wooden bench at the back of the room.
Joy followed him. He sat down and pulled her to him. "Are
you okay?"

"There are a lot of kids here." She chewed her thumbnail.

"I know, but soon they will all be your friends."

"I don't know." Uncertainty colored her shaky voice.

Anna Imhoff came in the door. She spied Joy and waved.
Joy waved back. Caleb said, "See, you have one friend here
already. Go and take your seat like the other children are
doing and listen to Leah. If you have a question, be sure and
raise your hand. I'll be right here if you need me."

"Promise?"

"I promise."

Joy walked reluctantly to her desk and sat down. Leah
went out and rang the school bell. The last students to come

in were the older boys who had been having a snowball fight outside. Tagging along behind them was David. He cast a curious look at Caleb and then raced to his seat.

When the clock at the front of the room reached eight-thirty, Leah tapped her desk bell with a pencil. The room instantly became quiet.

Leah scanned the room and recorded each of her students in her attendance book. Everyone was present.

She moved to the front of the classroom and smiled at all their bright and shining faces. "Good morning, boys and girls."

"Good morning, Leah," they replied in unison.

Walking to the blackboard, she wrote out the date followed by the arithmetic assignments for each of the classes as she did every morning. When she was finished, she returned to her desk and picked up her Bible.

Each day the teacher in an Amish school chose a passage to read. This morning Leah chose *Matthew* 5. When she finished reading the Sermon on the Mount, the students all rose, clasped their hands together and repeated the Lord's Prayer in unison. Joy, looking uncertain, stood, too, but she didn't know the words. It was another thing she would have to help her learn.

The Bible reading and prayer would be the only religious part of the day. The Amish believed that the instruction of faith was a sacred duty. Religion was taught at home and in their church services, not at school.

After everyone took their seats again, Leah glanced toward Caleb and gave him a tentative smile. She could see he was nervous about Joy's behavior. Neither one of them wanted to see Joy upset enough to have a tantrum.

She said, "Children, we have a new student joining us. This is Joy Perry. She is the granddaughter of Maggie and

Ike Mast. Her father, Caleb Mast, is also with us today. I want everyone to say good-morning to him."

The class turned in their seat and a chorus of greetings filled the schoolroom. He nodded to them. "Thank you."

Leah beckoned Joy to come forward. She rushed eagerly to Leah's side. It was a blessing that Joy had taken such a liking to her. It would make her transition into the community that much easier.

Leah said, "Joy comes to us from Houston, Texas. She grew up in an *Englisch* home. She doesn't speak our language, so please remember to speak English when you talk to her. I know everyone will make her feel welcome."

Joy smiled shyly at her new classroom and raised her hand in a quick wave. "Hi."

"Welcome, Joy." Anna Imhoff waved from her seat in the middle of the girls.

Leah leaned forward to see Joy's face. "Why don't you tell the children something about yourself?"

Joy looked up and whispered, "Like what?"

"Anything. You could tell them about Pickles."

Beaming, Joy said, "I have a puppy and her name is Pickles. She lives with her mommy at Leah's house, but when she is big enough, she will come live with me and she'll never, ever go away. Oh, and Dr. White says I have Up sindome, not Down sindome."

Leah nodded. "Very good. Anything else?"

Joy shook her head quickly, making the black ribbons of her *kapp* wiggle. She looked very Amish in her blue dress cut in the same style as the other girls. The Amish were all about uniformity and not standing out. The only difference between Joy and the other girls was that Joy's hair wasn't long enough yet to put into a braid or bun.

Leah picked up a copy of *Unpartheyisches Gesang-Buch,* their German songbook, from the corner of her desk. When she realized that Joy wouldn't know any of

the hymns, she laid it aside and picked up a collection of Christmas songs.

Singing was a normal part of each school day. Without being told, the children filed to the front of the room and lined up in their assigned places.

Joy stood to one side, not knowing where to go. Leah came to stand by her. She slipped her arm across Joy's shoulders. "It's Monday, and on Monday, Wednesday and Friday we normally sing German songs. The children take turns picking which songs we sing. Because it's your first day, how would you like to choose some Christmas songs to sing? Do you have a favorite?"

"'Up on the Rooftop.'"

"I'm afraid we don't have that one. What else do you like?"

"'Jingle Bells.'"

"We sing a song to that tune, but the words are different. I'm afraid you wouldn't know it." Leah realized it wasn't going as well as she had hoped.

"You pick a song." Joy was beginning to get frustrated.

"How about 'O Little Town of Bethlehem'? You were helping us sing it at your grandmother's house last Friday." Leah glanced toward Caleb and saw his tender smile. He remembered the evening, too.

Singing without accompaniment, the children blended their voices together in a spirited rendition of the chosen work. When the song was done, Leah helped Joy select two more. After they finished singing, she said, "Now I would like to run through the songs we have planned for the Christmas program. We will have a full rehearsal on Thursday after school, so everyone practice your parts for the plays and skits at home and be ready."

The songs included traditional Christmas hymns and popular secular songs that expressed the true meaning of Christmas. There was nothing about Santa or reindeer.

Only the first- and second-grade children had trouble with their song and had to repeat it several times. Joy listened but didn't join in. When they were done, Leah sent all her students back to their seats. They began working on their mathematics without urging from her.

With the upper grades working quietly, Leah gathered the first graders and Joy in a small group beside her desk where she could work with them on oral reading skills.

Like all Amish children, these first graders came to school speaking only Pennsylvania *Deitsh,* a German dialect outsiders called Pennsylvania Dutch.

English was the language of business and life outside the Amish home. It was essential that children learned to speak and write it. While the Amish strived to live separate from the world, they had to live in it. To that end, only English was spoken at school. Leah spoke Pennsylvania Dutch only when one of her young pupils didn't understand the meaning of what she was trying to express.

As Leah had suspected from Joy's sketchy records, the child couldn't read or write, but she seemed eager to learn. If she noticed that she was older than the other children, she didn't mention it. After they were finished, Leah had the first graders return to their seats and take out their workbooks to do the pages that corresponded with their reading lesson.

All the older students were working quietly, so she returned to help Joy copy the alphabet in her tablet. When the hour for arithmetic was up, the older students exchanged papers and graded each other's work. When each student had a chance to see their mistakes, the papers were passed to the front, where Leah collected them.

At ten o'clock, she said, "All right, children, it's time for recess. Go to the bathroom, get drinks of water and sharpen your pencils now so that you don't have to do it later."

The room dissolved into a beehive of activity as the

children put away their work and grabbed their coats to play outside.

Anna brought Emmy Chupp to Joy's desk. "This is Emmy. She wants to play Bear with us. Do you want to play?"

Joy looked eager to join them, but she held back. "I don't know that game."

"It's easy," Emmy said. "One of us is the bear and we try to catch someone else. Then they are the bear. It's fun, come on."

Caleb came forward. He said, "Don't forget to put on your coat."

"Will you watch me play Bear, Daddy?"

"That was my intention. Go on outside. I need to speak to Leah for a minute."

He waited until the last child was out the door before he spoke. "It seems to be going well, don't you think?"

"Did you expect it to go badly?"

"I had visions of screaming and temper tantrums. I'm happy to see I was wrong."

"The day isn't over yet." She walked to her desk and he joined her.

"What is your assessment of her learning readiness?"

She looked at him in surprise. "Don't you sound like a teacher?"

He flushed with embarrassment. "I'm doing my best to be an informed parent."

"I'm happy to see that. By this age, she should be in the second grade, but she is below the first-grade level in reading and comprehension. I don't believe her grandmother devoted much time to actual instructions. Joy is eager to learn, but she has a lot of catching up to do."

"What can I do to help her?"

"Work on reading. Read to her every night. Let her follow along with the words and repeat them after you. You

may want to teach her some of our German songs. That way she won't feel so left out during our morning singing. I'll give you a list of the ones that are easy."

"Good." He gestured toward the door. "I'd better get outside before recess is over. I don't want to miss seeing her be the bear."

Leah called to him before he reached the door. "Caleb, you are doing a good job with her. I see a lot of improvement in her behavior."

A wry smile pulled the corner of his mouth up. "You weren't with us when she jumped out of a moving buggy on the highway. She has a long way to go."

Leah hesitated to ask, but she wanted to know. "Does that mean you'll be staying longer than you thought?"

His smile widened. "I've found more than one reason to stick around."

He went out the door and Leah drew a sharp breath. Did he mean her? Had she given him the impression she would welcome his attentions? Her head told her no, but her heart disagreed.

At ten-fifteen, Leah rang the bell to bring the children back to class. Her grades four to eight had reading classes. Each student came and stood beside her, then read from their assignment and answered her questions to determine their comprehension of what they had read. All the time she was listening to her students, she was aware of Caleb sitting at the back of the room, watching her every move. She hadn't been this flustered since her first day as a teacher.

Eleven-thirty finally rolled around. She stood in front of her desk. "Children, you may go wash your hands, get your lunch boxes and return to your desks. Please go by rows. If any of the younger children need help, older brothers or sisters may go with them."

Joy fetched her lunch box and carried it to her father. "Can we go home now? I'm tired."

"School isn't over, Joy."

"But I want to go home now."

Caleb glanced at Leah. She came to sit beside him on the bench and spoke to Joy. "Are you feeling okay?"

Her lower lip stuck out. "I want to go home."

Leah met Caleb's gaze and raised her eyebrows. There wasn't any point in pushing the child to remain. He nodded in resignation.

Emmy ran up to Joy. "Don't go home yet. We're going to have another recess after we eat, and we can play on the swings. After that, we'll have story time and then we can color something. I'll let you use my crayons."

"You will?"

"*Ja,* I have lots of colors."

"Okay."

"What did you bring for lunch? My *mamm* sent me a roast beef sandwich and a big slice of carrot cake."

"*Mammi* gave me a peanut butter and jelly sandwich. I named Leah's puppies Pickles, Peanut Butter and Jelly." The two little girls walked back toward their seats.

Caleb blew out a breath of relief. "Crisis averted by crayons. Who knew they worked as well as animal crackers?"

They shared a smile, which sent a burst of happiness through Leah. He had a sense of humor, and she liked that about him. She liked a lot of things about Caleb Mast. But she couldn't sit here and flirt with him. She had a class to teach.

"Everyone back in your seats."

Joy opened her lunch box and was unwrapping her sandwich when Emmy stopped her. "We have to pray first."

Leah walked to the head of the class and clasped her hands together. The students repeated a prayer in unison and then quickly ate lunch. When they were done, they hurried outside. Caleb followed them out.

Leah made two cups of hot tea from the water in the

kettle and carried them outside along with her sandwich. She sat on the steps to keep an eye on the children. And on Caleb.

Caleb pushed Joy and Emmy on the swings, but the two girls soon decided they wanted to play on the teeter-totter. He saw Leah had come out of the building, and he crossed the schoolyard to join her on the steps. She inched a little farther away. He'd forgotten for a moment that there were many eyes on them.

He found her attractive, but he was beating his head against a closed door. They were separated by her sister's lies and so much more. Any feelings they had for each other were doomed before they could have the chance to explore them. She knew it as well as he did.

"I made you a cup of tea." She held out a mug.

"Danki." A strange yearning pulled at his insides. What would it be like if he wasn't *Englisch?* What if they could put the past behind them and start fresh? What if he made a home here with Joy? An Amish home. The image pulled at his soul and forced him to admit that he had been wrong to leave his faith behind along with his family.

The sun was bright overhead. It reflected off the snow in a million sparkling pinpoints of light. There was a chill in the air, but he endured it without complaint. For a little while, they sat quietly and watched the children on the playground. He was acutely aware that she was only inches away. He beat down the urge to reach for her hand.

She broke the silence first. "Joy seems to be doing better now."

His daughter was laughing as she rode up and down on the wooden teeter-totter. Anna was standing beside her. "I see she has made a friend. I've met Anna. Who is the other one?"

"Emmy Chupp."

"I don't think I know the family."

"The Chupps moved here last year. Her father works at the lumberyard. He fell and broke his leg a few weeks ago."

"I'm sorry to hear that. His daughter has taken quite a liking to Joy."

"Is that surprising?"

"Not at all. Even with the language barrier, she seems to be interacting well."

"Both Emmy and Anna have more experience speaking English. Emmy helps her mother and older sister in their soap-and-candle shop in town, so she speaks to many tourists. Anna's sister, Karen, married Jonathan Dresher, a convert to our faith. He credits Anna with teaching him our Pennsylvania Dutch language."

Caleb leaned back on his elbows and crossed his boots. "I've never known an outsider who chose to become Amish."

"You must ask him to tell you his story someday."

"I hope I have the chance to hear it."

She turned her head to frown at him. "You're not leaving yet, are you? Joy is not ready for that."

He wasn't ready for it, either. What he really wanted to know was Leah's feelings on the subject. "Will you miss me when I'm gone? Should I stay?"

He could tell he had flustered her. She stared at her hands wrapped around her mug of tea. When she wasn't looking, he had a chance to study the delicate curve of her neck and the rosy color in her cheeks. Did she have any idea how beautiful she was? He was glad she hadn't married his brother. He took a sip of tea and waited for her answer.

"I'm not sure that my opinion matters one way or the other."

"It does to me."

She sighed heavily. "What would you have me say? I am Amish, Caleb. You are not. I have taken my vows. If

nothing else stood between us, that would. I urge you to think of Joy. She has already lost or been abandoned by everyone she knows and loves. You're her father. She belongs with you."

"I am thinking of her. The longer I'm with her the less I want to go away and leave her here."

Leah placed a hand on his arm. "Then stay."

Chapter Twelve

Leah realized that Caleb was waiting for more encouragement from her. She was flattered that he cared for her. She cared for him, too. Perhaps more than she should, but she couldn't give him what he wanted.

She turned sideways on the step so she was facing him. "Caleb, if you stay or if you leave, it cannot be because of me. Would I like you to remain and become a part of our community? Of course. Your parents would, too. Many of your old friends would rejoice to know you have returned to us, but such a decision is too important to be made for one reason only. Pray for guidance. I will pray that you follow the path our Lord has chosen for you."

"Wise and kind as well as pretty. It's no wonder you are such a good teacher."

No man had called her pretty in a long time. His smile brought a warm glow to her heart. He truly had changed from the wild and reckless boy she once knew.

"Daddy, I found a cousin. I didn't know I had a cousin, did you?" Joy headed toward them, pulling David along by the hand.

Leah saw the sorrow that filled Caleb's eyes before he turned from her and gave his attention to the children. "I knew there was something I forgot to tell you."

She threw her arms around David in a bear hug. "This is David. His daddy is your brother, and that makes us cousins. I always wanted a cousin."

"Hello, David. It's nice to meet you."

David pulled away from Joy. "*Mamm* says not to speak to you."

Caleb nodded in resignation. "You are right to do what she tells you."

Leah rose from her place beside Caleb and took both Joy and David by the hand. "Did your *mamm* say you couldn't speak to Joy?"

"*Nee.*"

She began leading them toward the swing set. "Then you two must get to know each other. Why don't you push Joy on the swing and tell her all about your family and your home. David's father is your daddy's brother, but his mother is my sister. That makes David my nephew."

Joy tipped her head sideways as she gazed up at Leah. "Does that make you my aunt?"

"*Nee,* it makes me David's aunt. We say *aenti*. You and I are not related at all."

Joy looked disappointed. "I never had an *aenti* before."

David brightened. "You do have one. My *mamm* is your *aenti*."

"She is?"

Leah nodded. "Rhonda is your *aenti,* and her husband, Wayne, is your *onkel,* your uncle."

Joy's face grew troubled. "Mama used to tell me her boyfriends were my uncles. I didn't like them. Sometimes they were mean."

"My *daed* is not mean. You would like him. He takes me sledding and ice skating in the winter, and he lets me help him drive the team of horses during the summer."

"He doesn't sound mean. I might like him."

David pointed toward a farm in the distance. "That's our *haus*."

"What does that mean?"

Leah translated. "It means *house*. That's where David and his parents live."

Joy shaded her eyes to look into the distance. "That's not so far."

"It only takes me ten minutes to walk to school. I have a brown-and-white pony named Budget. He's really fast."

Joy grinned. "I like horses. Can I meet him?"

"I don't know. Mom doesn't like your dad."

Leah looked over her shoulder. Caleb rose from his seat and entered the school. Once again, she was struck by how alone he seemed to be. She prayed God would show her the way to heal the breach between their families.

Caleb had come to school to make sure that Joy felt comfortable in the new surroundings. Although his main reason for being in the building was to keep an eye on his daughter, he found his gaze constantly drawn to Leah. He watched the way she moved, the way she gestured with her hands when she spoke, the way she seemed genuinely interested in every student in her classes. It was clear that her students adored her in return. The entire room was well behaved and respectful.

After their conversation on the steps, he was pleased to know she wasn't indifferent to him, but he also knew their relationship wouldn't go forward until he made a major commitment.

He wasn't sure he could do it. Coming back to the Amish had not been on his to-do list. But then, neither had becoming a father to Joy. The Lord's path for him was taking some strange twists and turns. Leah was right. Remain-

ing in Hope Springs wasn't something he could decide on his own. He needed divine guidance. He might be rusty at praying, but he still knew how to do it.

Please, Lord, show me the path You would have me take and give me the courage to follow it.

At three-thirty, Leah addressed the school. "On Wednesday, the day after tomorrow, we are going to do a special project. We are going to make a feast for our feathered friends. When the snow is deep, the birds have difficulty finding food. Since Christmas is just around the corner, I thought we should lend them a helping hand. I have made a list of things I would like you to bring to school."

She moved down the rows, handing out note cards. When she reached the back, where Caleb was seated, she handed him a card, too. He turned it over. It said, *This way, you will have many hands to help make your decorations.*

She walked back to the front of the room. "You are dismissed. I will see you all tomorrow."

Caleb walked forward through the stream of children headed out the door. He helped Joy gather her things and stow them in her desk. "What did you think of your first day of school?"

"I like recess."

"That was my favorite part of school, too." He was grateful that she had managed the entire day without a meltdown and had made a few friends in the process.

Leah straightened up the classroom and erased the problems from the blackboard. "Tomorrow will be even more fun."

Joy gaped at her. "I have to come here *again?*"

Caleb laughed. "Only until you finish the eighth grade."

She shut her desk. "I hope that doesn't take very long. Leah, can you walk home with us?"

Bless you, child, you took the words right out of my mouth. Caleb waited with bated breath for Leah to answer.

"Since we both are going in the same direction, I don't see why not."

"Cool."

Caleb made sure Joy was bundled up against the cold and that he had his rising excitement in check. Just because Leah agreed to walk a little ways with Joy didn't mean she wanted to walk out with him.

Leah closed the school door behind them and tied her bonnet under her chin. "I think we are in for more snow."

Caleb glanced at the low gray clouds scuttling by. "You may be right."

They fell into step together as they started down the path through the woods. It would have been almost as easy to reach Leah's house by walking along the road, but the quiet stillness of the trees offered privacy and a feeling of intimacy.

When Joy ran a little ways ahead of them along the path, Leah asked quietly, "Are you seriously considering staying in Hope Springs?"

He wished he could tell what she was thinking. "I have started to think that it might be an option."

"What has changed your mind?"

He wanted to say she had, but he didn't. "Many things, but mostly it's because I have missed all of Joy's life up until now. I don't want to miss more."

"I can understand that. It won't be easy if you do stay."

"I know. I have to find a way to make it work, if that exists. Wayne and Rhonda are dead set against my staying."

"Perhaps they will come around in time."

"Maybe. Do you think they will? You know them better than I do." He took a huge leap of faith and reached for her hand.

* * *

Startled, Leah almost pulled away, but she didn't. He slowed his steps and so did she. She wasn't in any hurry to reach the place where they would part ways.

Remembering Rebecca's words about how God had used her as a tool to bring Gideon back to his faith, Leah wondered if God wanted to use her in the same fashion to help Caleb.

It was a fine line to walk. She would have to guard her heart against caring too much for a man who was forbidden.

She thought about his question and finally said, "Rhonda carries so much bitterness in her heart. I don't know if she will ever be able to see past that."

"Can you?"

"The past can't be changed. It is what we do in the present that matters. Can you leave the English world and all its temptations behind?"

"Can I live Amish again? Maybe."

"I fear there's not much conviction in your voice."

"You're right. I have doubts, but I'm open to the idea. I couldn't have said that two weeks ago. I'm praying about it, and I couldn't have said that two weeks ago, either."

"Then I will pray you make the right decision."

Joy came running up and squeezed in between them. She took each of their hands. Leah shared a smile with Caleb as Joy began to chatter about the things she enjoyed doing with her new friends at school.

Leah tempered her rising happiness with a heavy dose of practicality. Many things stood between them, and she wasn't at all sure of what God wanted from her.

"Joy, is your daddy taking you to see the Christmas parade in Hope Springs on Saturday?"

Joy grinned at her dad. "Can we go to the Christmas parade? Please, please, please?"

Caleb rolled his eyes. "Now that Leah has mentioned it, I'm pretty sure that you will bug me until I do. Since when has Hope Springs sponsored a Christmas parade?"

"This will be our first annual Christmas parade. It was the brainchild of the new mayor. Tourism falls off in the winter months. He thought a Christmas parade might bring more people to town and give a boost to the local economy."

"It's a good idea, if the weather cooperates. What is the forecast for Saturday?"

"The paper said it will be sunny but cold. Still, it could be worse. Everyone is looking forward to the event."

"Are you going to be there?" Joy asked.

"I am going with my sister and her family."

"Oh." Joy's lower lip stuck out as she pouted. "I wanted you to go with us."

"I am sure that we will see each other there."

"That's not the same. You don't like me anymore." Joy let go of their hands and ran toward home.

Leah called after, but she didn't look back.

Caleb said, "Don't worry. She gets cranky like this when she gets tired, and she has had a long day."

Leah felt terrible for upsetting her. "I will remember that and make sure that she takes a rest break at school."

"I should keep her in sight so she doesn't get lost. See you tomorrow." He followed his daughter, leaving Leah watching them and wondering if Joy would ever gain the sense of security and confidence that she needed.

The following morning proved to be a difficult one for both Leah and Joy. Emmy Chupp's mother arrived for a visit and brought fresh baked cupcakes for the class because it was Emmy's birthday. She sat quietly at the back of the room just as Caleb was doing. Joy became increasingly restless throughout the morning and had trouble staying on track.

She frequently got up from her desk and disrupted the

other children who were trying to work. At recess, she refused to play with the other children and remained at her desk. Emmy's mother went home after she distributed the cupcakes at lunch. When she was gone, Joy went out to play, and Leah held a short conference with Caleb.

"What am I doing wrong?" She was seated behind her desk, feeling worn-out and frustrated.

He rested his hip casually against one corner of the desk. "I don't think we're doing anything wrong. Joy has trouble adjusting to change. I think once she becomes used to a routine, her behavior will improve."

"The teacher is the one who is supposed to be encouraging the parent, not the other way around."

"We are both finding our way with her. My one consolation is that her life here is so much better than when she was with her mother."

Leah moved a set of papers from one side of her desk to the other. "Have you heard anything from her mother?"

"Not a word. My attorney let me know that my petition for full custody has been granted. It will take more time to have Valerie's parental rights severed permanently."

"Has Joy spoken about her?"

"Not since the evening we left your place and she jumped out of the buggy on the way home. Do you think I should talk to her about Valerie?"

"I don't know. On one hand, I think it would be good for her to share what she's feeling, but on the other hand, I don't want to upset her more than she already is."

"I feel the same way. If she continues to misbehave this afternoon, how would you feel if I took her out of school and took her home?"

"You are her father. You are the best one to make that decision."

"You are forgetting that I've only been a father for two

months. I'm not sure you can make a case that I'm the best one to make decisions for her."

"Who else is there?"

"Good point. Honestly, Leah, if you see me taking the wrong track with her, let me know."

He was deadly serious. She had an overwhelming urge to wrap her arms around him and tell him that he was doing a fine job. He had been given a difficult task, and he was trying his best to do the right thing for his child. "It's good to know that you are open to suggestions. Not all of my fathers are."

He glanced at the clock. "Time to round them up."

"Let us pray that the afternoon goes better."

He stood up. "Amen to that."

Their prayers were answered. Joy came in from playing outside, hung up her coat and mittens, and calmly took her seat. For the rest of the afternoon, she was a model student. Leah exchanged a puzzled glance with Caleb. He simply shrugged his shoulders. Neither one of them knew what had changed.

On Wednesday, Joy was up early and dressed for school by the time Caleb came down for breakfast. She had finished setting plates on the table. "What should I do now, *Mammi?*"

Caleb took his place at the table. His father had already eaten and had gone out to do chores. His mother smiled at Joy. "You can fetch the butter from the refrigerator and then we are ready to eat."

Joy did as she was asked, and then took a seat at the table and folded her hands. "I am ready to pray, Daddy."

He shared an amused look with his mother, then said, "We normally say our prayers silently, but since you do not know them, I will teach this to you."

He bowed his head and closed his eyes. Joy did the same.

"This is the *Gebet Nach Dem Essen,* the Prayer Before Meals. Lord God, heavenly Father, bless us and these Thy gifts, which we accept from Thy tender goodness. Give us food and drink for our souls unto life eternal, that we may share Thy heavenly table with Thee, through Jesus Christ. Amen."

He then recited the Lord's Prayer as was done before every meal. When he finished, he opened his eyes and looked at Joy. She still had her eyes scrunched closed and her hands folded.

Caleb's mother came up behind him and placed a kiss on the top of his head, something she hadn't done since he was seven years old. "You may eat now, both of you."

Joy's eyes popped open and she grabbed her fork. "*Goot,* because I'm hungry. We're going to do something fun in school today. We are going to make things for the birds to eat."

Caleb's mother dished up the food and then took a seat beside her granddaughter. "So you like school, do you?"

"Mostly. I like recess the best. I like my teacher, and I like Emmy, and Anna and David. They are my friends."

She cocked her head to the side and looked at her grand-mother. "It's okay to be friends with my cousin, isn't it?"

"It is most definitely okay," Maggie assured her.

Joy finished eating in record time and waited impatiently for Caleb to get done. When they were finally on the way to school, he tentatively broached the subject of her mother.

"Have you mailed all the Christmas cards that you made the other night?"

"Yup."

"Did you make one for your mother?"

"Yeah, but I don't think she'll get it. I don't know where she lives now. *Mammi* wrote Nana's address on it."

"Maybe your step-grandpa will give it to her."

"I don't think so. He didn't like her. He called her a junkie."

"Do you know what that means?"

"It means she gets sick, and she has to take really bad medicine, but it never makes her better."

"I guess that's about right."

"She could get better if she wants to. Nana said that. But I don't think Mama wants to."

"From now on, when we say our prayers at night, we are going to ask God to help her get better."

"Do you think He can do that?"

"Yes. I believe He can."

The rest of the morning went off without a hitch. Joy repeated much of the Lord's Prayer with the other children and joined in singing some of the songs she had learned. She wrote out all the letters of the alphabet and happily showed them to Leah. She was behaving so well that he began to think they were over the hump at school and she could do without him. When the children went out for their first recess, he mentioned the idea to Leah. She agreed it was worth a try.

He waited until the children were going out for their lunch recess before he pulled Joy aside. Leah came to stand beside them. He was grateful for her presence.

"Joy, I want to talk to you."

"But, Daddy, it's time for recess."

"You can go in a minute. Remember I told you I would always let you know when I was leaving and when I would be back?"

"Kind of." She tipped her head slightly as she stared out at the children playing in the schoolyard.

"Okay. I wanted to let you know that I'm going home for a little while this afternoon to help Grandpa. I will be back before school lets out so we can walk home together. Is that okay?"

"Sure. Can I go play now?"

So much for the meltdown that he had been expecting. He exchanged glances with Leah. She looked as relieved as he felt. "Okay. Have a good time. I'll see you later."

She ran out to join the circle of children getting ready to play Duck, Duck, Goose. Anna Imhoff and David made room for her between them.

Caleb blew out a breath and walked to the door. "That was easier than I thought it would be."

"She seems to be adjusting well. She's a different child than the one you brought to school yesterday."

"I think so, too."

They stepped outside and stood close together on the steps of the school. He was reluctant to leave. If Joy did well, he would lose his excuse to spend time with Leah.

"I will keep a close eye on her," she assured him.

Caleb allowed his gaze to linger on her face. "I know that. I couldn't ask for a more capable or compassionate teacher for Joy. You've been good for her. And for me."

A blush stained her cheeks and she looked away.

Realizing he had said too much, he walked down the steps and started toward home.

Leaving Joy at school was much harder than Caleb had expected. At the edge of the woods, he stopped and looked back. Leah still stood on the steps, watching him. He lifted a hand in a brief wave. She did the same. It wasn't much, but somehow it raised his spirits immensely.

When he reached the house, he saw a buggy tied to the gate and recognized Wayne's horse. He half hoped that Rhonda had come to visit his mother. Maybe he could convince her to tell the truth now.

He was disappointed to see his brother come out the front door. Wayne folded his arms over his chest. "I would speak with you."

"Fine. Say what you have to say. I'm listening."

Wayne looked over his shoulder toward the house. "Not here. Get in the buggy."

Caleb extended his arm. "After you."

Both men climbed into the buggy. Wayne picked up the reins and sent the horse trotting out of the yard. Caleb waited until they were at the end of the lane before he spoke again. "I want to thank you for agreeing to let Joy attend school at Walnut Valley."

"My wife insisted."

"Then please give her my thanks."

"You have what you came for. Why are you still here?"

"I came because I wanted to see Joy settled and happy. The longer I'm around her, the less anxious I am to leave. She is my daughter, after all."

"There are people in the church who believe our parents are wrong to allow you to stay. There's talk of shunning them."

"Is that why we're taking this little ride? So you can guilt me into leaving. Again."

Wayne turned the horse into a cornfield and pulled to a stop. "We all know you left to be with your *Englisch* girlfriend."

"You don't really think I left because of Valerie, do you? I will admit that Valerie made leaving easier, but she wasn't the reason I couldn't stay."

"You left because you couldn't face what you had done to Rhonda. She is a good woman. She deserved better from you."

"She did deserve better from someone. Just not from me. I dated her for a while because I felt sorry for her after the accident, but I was never with her in that way. I left because no one believed my side of the story. Not even you. After what I did for you, how could you turn your back on me that way?"

"Lying comes easy to you."

"And silence comes easily to you. A lie doesn't have to be spoken to be a lie. Why haven't you told Rhonda that you were driving the car that hit her that night? I can understand why you never admitted it to our parents. Dad thinks the sun rises and sets on you. You were always the good son. I knew it would break his heart to find out you ran away and left an injured woman trapped under that car."

"Your car! The forbidden thing you kept hidden in the woods. You made me drive it. It was all your fault," Wayne shouted. "I never would have gone to such a party without you egging me on. Laughing at me, poking fun at me, calling me a coward. You led me astray. God forgive me."

Caleb stared down at his hands. "I know I did. That's why I let everyone believe I was driving. They were shocked but not surprised. They expected trouble from me."

"Go away. Haven't you done enough?"

Yes, and I've suffered enough, too, brother. I want a new start. You owe me that.

He didn't say what he was thinking. Instead, he looked at Wayne. "You have been married to Rhonda for nine years. How can you look at her every day and not tell her the truth about that night?"

Wayne seemed to shrink in on himself. "At first, Rhonda said she forgave you. I thought things would be all right for her. Then she became pregnant and you refused to marry her. She was crushed. She changed. She became a different woman.

"It was only after we wed that I saw how much she hates the way she looks. She can't bear to have people stare at her. She has never forgiven the person who scarred her. To this day, she carries that bitterness in her heart. How could I admit that I am the one responsible after she believed it was you for so long?"

Caleb realized he wasn't the only one suffering because of the deceit they had carried out. He didn't want to feel

sorry for his brother, but he heard the despair in Wayne's voice. Was there any way to help?

He laid a hand on Wayne's arm. "Swallowed alive by guilt and bitterness is a terrible way to live. Have you thought about getting some professional help? Dr. White is a good man. He can find someone that you can talk to. Someone who can help Rhonda find a way to accept her disfigurement."

Wayne stiffened and shook off Caleb's hand. "We will not air our dirty laundry in public. We did well enough until you came back. We will do well enough when you are gone." He slapped the reins against the horse's rump, drove back out onto the highway and headed toward the farm.

"And if I decide not to leave?" Caleb asked.

Wayne looked shocked. "What are you saying?"

"I'm considering returning to the Amish."

"No!"

"You don't get a say in how I live my life from now on."

"The church congregation must vote to accept your return. They won't. Not if I can help it. There is no repentance in your heart. I will say this to all."

Caleb struggled to control his temper. "There are other congregations in the area. You can't keep me out of them all."

Wayne pulled to a stop in front of Ike's house. "Have you come back to torment me?"

"No, I came home because I have a daughter with Down syndrome. She needs a loving home and a welcoming community to live in. I thought I would find that here. You have son. You know what I'm talking about."

Wayne's anger drained away. "My wife is afraid of you. Somehow, she believes you can hurt David."

"I won't. I promise you that."

"I know what it is to love a child. I could not love him more if he were mine."

"Then for the sake of our children and our parents, let us find a way to be civil to one another."

Before Wayne could answer, a teenage boy came running up to the buggy. He leaned on the wheel to catch his breath. "Teacher sent me to find you, Caleb Mast. Joy has run away."

Chapter Thirteen

Leah went weak with relief when she saw Caleb leap out of the buggy that came tearing into the schoolyard. The feeling was quickly followed by shame. She ran toward him and threw herself into his arms. "I am so sorry."

He hugged her close. "Have you found her?"

"*Nee.* I have the older children scouring the woods. They are to listen for the school bell. If it rings, they are to come back."

"What happened?"

"I don't know. Everything seemed to be going fine. She was happily playing with the others. I went inside to write out the history assignment for the upper grades. I was only gone a few minutes. I rang the bell to call everyone inside, and that's when I noticed she wasn't with the other children."

Leah was shocked to see Wayne get out of the buggy, as well. "Is there someplace she might go?"

Caleb turned in a circle as he raked a hand through his hair. "She's not familiar with anything but the way to get to school and the way to go home. Leah, is it possible she went to your house to see the puppy?"

Leah hated the look of fear on his face. She hated know-

ing she was responsible. "I sent two of my girls to check. They aren't back yet."

"If she's not there, I have no idea where she can be. Are you sure none of the children saw where she went? Were there any cars that stopped on the road?"

Leah shook her head. "The children saw nothing out of the ordinary."

"She couldn't have vanished into thin air." His frustration was breaking through.

Leah saw the girls she had sent to her house running toward her. They didn't have Joy with them. They stopped beside her. "We didn't see any sign of her."

"*Danki,* please go inside and help watch the little ones."

Wayne said, "We can organize a bigger search party and get some men on horseback to cover more ground. Ring the bell, Leah, and call the children back. We will send them home and have their fathers meet us here."

"Please, God, let her be all right." Caleb walked away from the school and began calling her name. Leah had been doing it to no avail.

She hurried to the school bell and began ringing it. One by one, the children returned from the wooded area and fields next to the school. As the last one came in, Leah noticed a pony cart coming down the road. She recognized her sister. A moment later, she realized Rhonda wasn't alone. Joy sat beside her.

Leah screamed to Caleb, "We found her."

He ran to her side. "Where is she?"

Leah pointed toward the road. "She is with my sister."

Rhonda turned her pony into the schoolyard and stopped. Caleb snatched Joy off the seat and held her tight. "Thank God you are safe."

"Daddy, you are squishing me."

He dropped to one knee and set her on her feet in front

of him. "You have to stop scaring me like this. Why did you run away?"

"I didn't run away. I went to David's house to meet my *aenti* and to see his pony. Can I have a pony, please? I'll take good care of it."

Leah knelt beside them. "Joy, you can't leave school without permission."

"I can't? Why not?"

"Because that is the rule," Leah said.

"That's just silly."

Caleb stood and looked down at her. "It is not silly. It is the rule. And you are never again to leave without permission. Do you understand?

Her lower lip stuck out. "Yes, Daddy."

Caleb offered his hand to Leah and helped her to her feet. He turned to Rhonda. "Thank you for the care you have shown my daughter."

She looked away. Without a word, she turned the pony and drove away. Wayne went inside the school and returned a moment later with David. "Get in the buggy, *sohn*."

Joy waved at David. "I like your pony."

Leah met Caleb's glance. "Why don't you take Joy home, too? I'm letting school out early. I think we have all had enough excitement for one day."

"But what about the bird treats we were going to make?" Joy asked.

Leah smiled at her. "We will make them first thing tomorrow morning. How will that be?"

"Goot!" she shouted.

Caleb gave his daughter a small push toward the school. "Go get your things."

As she ran up the steps, Leah turned to Caleb. "I am so sorry that this happened. Please forgive me."

He drew her close and wrapped his arms around her. "There is nothing to forgive. I have the feeling that life

with Joy is always going to be an adventure. I just thank God that she is okay."

Leah knew she should move out of his embrace, but nothing had ever felt so right or so comforting. "I shouldn't have let it happen. I should've kept a closer eye on her." She pressed her face against his neck.

He cupped her cheek with his hand. "You were as frightened as I was. I see how much you care for my child. I hope you know how much she cares for you. Almost as much as I do."

Leah raised her face and looked into his eyes. They were filled with tenderness. She knew that he was going to kiss her. She knew she should stop him, but she didn't.

The gentle touch of his lips sent a thrill straight through her. The moment was everything she had dreamed it would be and more. Her heart skipped a beat and soared with happiness.

He drew away suddenly. "I have wanted to do that for a very long time."

She stepped out of his arms as reality brought her crashing back to earth. She hoped none of her students had been watching. "It doesn't change things. You know that."

"It does for me. You are making a hard decision much easier. Bless you, Leah, you are a rare treasure."

The schoolhouse door opened and Joy came out with her lunch box and the paper she had finished that day.

"Look what I did, *Daed*. I want to show *Mammi* I got 100 on my math paper."

"That's great, honey. Say goodbye to your teacher, and let's go home."

As they walked away, Leah realized she had been wrong. The kiss did change things. She could never look at him again without remembering it. It was a memory she would hold close to her heart.

* * *

"You look happy today, teacher."

Leah realized she was grinning foolishly and schooled her expression into something more appropriate for the classroom. Anna, Emmy, David and Kyle were gathered in front of her desk. "I'm happy because Christmas is almost here."

And because Caleb Mast had kissed her yesterday.

It had been all too brief, but that hadn't detracted from its impact. She started smiling again just thinking about the tender way his lips brushed hers. She would remember forever the sweetness of the moment.

Anna said, "Christmas is what we wanted to talk to you about. Actually, about our Christmas program."

"What about our program?" The rehearsal had gone quite well. Only one child had forgotten his lines.

"Joy doesn't have a part in it," Kyle said.

Everyone but Joy had remained after school for the rehearsal. She had gone home with her father after having an entire day that was crisis-free.

Leah frowned slightly. "Joy started school so late that I didn't think she would have time to learn our songs or a part in the play or the skits you children are putting on. I don't want to make her feel uncomfortable. I thought it would be best if she watched the program with her family this year. I promise that next year we will include her."

Anna looked at her friends and then said, "We have written a play for her. I know that it's your job to choose the songs and plays, but maybe this once we could do one?"

What wonderful children they were for wanting to include Joy. "I'm pleased that you have thought of this. But the programs have already been printed."

"Couldn't you just announce that we have added one more play?" Anna handed Leah a piece of paper.

Leah opened it and read the short play. She looked at the children standing in front of her as her heart swelled with happiness. "Are you sure you want to try this?"

They all nodded vigorously.

"All right. I will talk to Joy's father and grandmother and find out if they can help her learn her part."

"*Danki,* teacher. We will help her, too," Kyle said. He knew how hard it was to be an outsider coming into a small Amish community. It was generous of him to help make Joy's transition easier.

The children finished straightening up the desks and went home. Leah stayed behind to finish her own work. Picking up an eraser, she began to clean the blackboard. Now that she was alone, she was free to think about "the kiss" and what it might mean for her if Caleb stayed and joined the church.

Laying down the eraser, she picked up a piece of chalk and wrote *Caleb Mast* in large letters across the board. Then beneath it she added *Mrs. Caleb Mast,* then *Mr. and Mrs. Caleb Mast.*

She stared at the board and started to giggle. She wasn't any better than the boy-crazy girls in her eighth-grade class. The possibility of marriage and family made Leah's heart sing, but she was a practical woman, not a teenage girl. One kiss did not mean a lifetime together.

Caleb hadn't said anything about love or marriage. Although he was considering returning to the Amish way of life, he had not yet made that commitment. A kiss was just a kiss without it. But if he chose not to stay, her heart would break in a million pieces.

On Saturday, she would spend the day with her sister and her family. While Caleb had made strides in repairing his relationship with his parents, he hadn't made any progress in gaining her sister's forgiveness. Although Caleb was a touchy subject, Leah hoped that she could find a

way to help Rhonda accept, if not welcome, his return to the community.

She stared at the blackboard and sighed. She was letting her foolish heart put the cart before the horse. She picked up the eraser again and wiped away her daydreams.

If the new mayor's goal was to bring people to Hope Springs for the Christmas parade, the plan was a whopping success. Caleb held Joy's hand as they made their way along Main Street. His parents walked behind them. The parade wasn't due to start for another half hour, but already there were crowds of people seated on lawn chairs lining the street. The mix was equally Amish and non-Amish. There were sheriff's deputies and town police officers directing traffic away from Main Street to keep it open for the parade vehicles. Caleb had left their buggy at the parking lot next to the Wadler Inn, near the edge of town.

"Where are we going to sit, Daddy?" Joy tried to see around the people in front of them.

He was searching the crowd for Leah, but he hadn't seen her or his brother. He looked over his shoulder. "Where do you think, *Daed?*"

"Down by the park. There is more space and we will be able to see more than just this narrow street."

"The park it is." Caleb moved ahead quickly. If Leah was here, he wanted to see her. He didn't have to speak to her, although he would like that very much. But just to see her would be enough today.

It was hard to stop thinking about her. About the kiss they had shared. Did she regret it? Had he embarrassed her? Would she let him kiss her again? They were questions he was afraid to ask. He knew if they saw each other, he would read the answers on her face.

His father was right. People were more spread out along the edge of the park. A number of children were making

good use of the playground. He and his father set out their canvas folding chairs while his mother unpacked food from a small basket. As soon as they were settled, she handed out whoopee pies and bottled drinks.

Caleb was amazed at the number of people who stopped to say hello and to meet Joy. He had dressed Plain that day, with the dark coat, dark pants and black wide-brimmed hat borrowed from his father. They had been sitting for about ten minutes when Joy suddenly bolted out of her chair and ran toward an English family. He rushed after her as she grabbed a little girl about her own age and squealed with glee.

"I'm sorry," he said to the startled father.

"Look, Daddy. She's just like me."

It was then Caleb realized the other child also had Down syndrome. Her father extended his hand. "I see you are blessed with a special child, too. Aren't they amazing children?"

"Yes. I hope she didn't frighten your daughter. She doesn't normally grab people. Joy, let her go, honey."

"Melissa hugs everyone. I'm Gerard Franks. Do you live in the area?"

"Joy and I recently moved to Hope Springs. I'm Caleb Mast."

"Nice to meet you. We live near Millersburg. Not too far away. Maybe we can get together for a playdate with our girls one of these days."

"I think Joy would like that."

Gerard pulled out a business card. "I'm the treasurer of the local Down syndrome support group. We meet once a month so that our families can get together and enjoy each other's company."

"I didn't realize there was a support group for children like Joy."

Gerard looked surprised. "There are local as well as

national chapters. If you're interested, drop by one of our meetings. We're working to change the world's perception of our children and give them the future they deserve. We also help new parents face the special challenges our blessings bring. We have many Amish families in our group. Joy won't feel out of place."

He took his daughter's hand and they walked away. Joy turned to Caleb. "She has Up sindome just like me."

"I see that."

He stared at the card in his hand. It felt strange to know other people were dealing with the same issues that he faced. That they were working to ensure the same kind of future for their children that he was seeking for Joy. Somehow, he thought such acceptance only happened among the Amish. It seemed that he was wrong. If things didn't work out, if he found he couldn't accept the Amish way of life again, he and Joy wouldn't have to face life alone.

He walked back to his parents and held Joy on his lap so that she could see better. The shrill siren announced the beginning of the parade. Leading the way was the county sheriff's SUV with all its lights flashing. As it rolled down the street, the siren would sound every few minutes. Joy got off his lap and raced to the edge of the street. She covered her ears and grinned each time the siren sounded.

Walking behind the sheriff's vehicle was a color guard made up of veterans. They held their flags stiffly in front of them and marched with precision. Some of them were older than Caleb's father.

After that came the high school marching band, a saddle club with all the horses sporting red-and-white ribbons braided into their manes and tails, and numerous homemade floats from the local merchants and churches. Some of the car dealerships from as far away as New Philadelphia had convertibles and trucks decked out with holiday lights and Christmas trees. They threw candy toward the

children gathered along the edge of the street as a fellow dressed like Santa Claus rode up and down and all around on a small motor scooter.

When the local ambulance passed by, Caleb caught sight of Leah and her family on the other side of the street. David saw Joy at the same time and darted out into the street toward her.

He didn't see the motor scooter bearing down on him. Santa was waving to the crowd and didn't notice the boy in his path.

Caleb shot into the street, but a sheriff's deputy had already grabbed David and hauled him out of harm's way.

Caleb and Rhonda reached him at the same time. There was something familiar about the man, but Caleb couldn't place him. The officer tipped his hat toward Rhonda. "Long time no see, Rhonda."

The color leached out of her face. She reached for David, but the officer held on to him. The officer's eyes never left Rhonda's face. "You've got a nice-looking boy, Rhonda."

She reached out and yanked her son away from him. He smiled as she hurried back into the crowd. Caleb had a chance to study him. The uniform was different from those of the officers he had seen directing traffic. The patch on his arm bore the logo of the county to the south.

When the man turned toward Caleb, he realized who it was. Drake Colburn, the deputy on the scene the night of Rhonda's accident. He looked Caleb up and down. "What do you want?"

"Just to add my thanks. How do you know my brother's wife?"

"That's my business and none of yours. Have a nice day." He walked away along the parade route, motioning to people to move back out of the street.

Caleb returned to his family. The parade was soon over and they joined the flow of the crowd as they headed out of

town. He scanned the area for Leah but didn't see her. She would be at the church service tomorrow. It was unlikely that they would find time to be alone together, but tomorrow night they had something special planned for Joy. He knew he'd have the chance to repeat their kiss or discover if he was wasting his time. He walked on, disappointed but more than a little curious about Rhonda's reaction to Drake Colburn.

On the way to the buggy, Joy stopped to stare in the window of a shop with a white flocked tree on display. She pressed her nose to the glass. "It's a pretty tree. Mama said we would have one like this someday."

He didn't know what to say. He took her hand and gently led her away. "Did you like the parade?"

She looked over her shoulder. Another family had stopped in front of the window to admire the display. "Christmas is for families to be together."

"Yes, it is. And I'm glad I have you with me this Christmas. You are making it very special. You are my very own Christmas Joy."

She smiled at him then, and he hoped the tree and thoughts of her mother would be forgotten.

Caleb had made up his mind, but he was still nervous as he rode in the buggy with his parents and Joy on Sunday morning. If he was coming back to the Amish community, and back to God, attending church was the best place to start. Then a job would be next on his list. He couldn't live on his savings forever.

"It will be *goot* to have our son and granddaughter listen to the Lord's words with us." His mother could not have looked more pleased. Even his father was in a happy mood. He let Joy take the reins for a while as they trotted along a deserted stretch of country road.

It didn't take long to reach the Yutzi farmstead, where

the services were to be held. Caleb unhitched the horse and led it to a nearby corral where two dozen other horses were lined up in their harnesses, munching on hay and waiting to make the return trip with their families. When he approached the barn where the preaching was to take place, he saw that his parents and Joy had already gone in.

He stepped inside the cavernous opening. Tarps had been used to cover the hay bales stacked along each side. The benches had been set out in rows with a wide center aisle. The men sat on one side and the women sat on the other.

Caleb walked to the last row. A pair of teenage boys scooted over to make room for him. He was prepared to spend three hours sitting on a hard wooden bench. What he wasn't prepared for was the swelling emotion that engulfed him when the first familiar hymn began.

The slow and mournful chanting rose in volume as many voices blended in the ancient German song that had been passed down through the generations. No music accompanied the singing. Only the voices of the faithful poured into his ears and into his heart.

Listening to the words of sorrow, hope and God's promise of salvation, Caleb felt a stirring deep within his soul. Why had he stayed away from God so long? His life had been empty without faith, but God was filling him again.

He quietly added his voice to the chorus. When the song was done, he listened intently to Bishop Zook as he spoke about the hardship of the journey that Joseph and Mary had undergone on the way to Bethlehem and the great joy that awaited them at journey's end.

When the second hymn began, Caleb opened the hymnal beside him on the bench and joined in the song. He looked across the aisle and saw Leah looking his way. She smiled at him, and it turned his heart inside out. He suddenly realized he didn't just like her. He was falling in love with

her. With her kindness, her wonderful bright mind and her adorable smile.

God had given him a special daughter, and Joy had led him home, to his family and to his faith. Had God used Joy to bring him love, too? Did the Lord have more blessings in store for him?

Caleb opened his heart and prayed that Leah would be one of them.

Much later that afternoon, Caleb sat at the kitchen table and motioned to his parents that he was leaving the house. They smiled and his father winked at him, as happy as a kid to be in on the secret.

Caleb said, "Joy, I have a surprise for you."

"What is it?"

"If I told you, it wouldn't be a surprise. Put your coat, snow pants, boots and mittens on."

"Why?"

"Because your surprise is outside."

She took her coat from the peg and buttoned it. "Is it big? Is it a pony? Is it a sled?"

"It's not a pony or a sled. Stop asking questions and hurry up." He opened the door. She pulled on her snow pants and boots and joined him. He led her along the path they took to school.

When they were at the place where the path made a small bend, he said, "Cover your eyes and no peeking."

She placed her mittens over her face. "I can't see."

He picked her up and carried her the rest of the way.

"Can I look now?"

"No. Keep those peepers shut." It was a bit of a struggle to walk through the thick snow, but he trudged ahead.

She waited another minute. "Can I look now?"

"I guess so." He was standing in front of her tree.

Her eyes opened wide with shock. "A Christmas tree." Her voice was hushed with wonder.

Leah stepped out from behind it. "Surprise. Do you like it?"

Joy threw her arms around Caleb's neck and squeezed hard as she pressed a kiss to his cheek.

His heart swelled with love. "I guess that means you like it."

"It's beautiful." She struggled to get down. He set her on her feet in the deep snow. Leah had tied red bows of yarn to the branches. With the newly fallen snow clinging to the needles, it looked sparkling and bright. Joy walked around the tree and clapped her hands.

Leah smiled at him. The sight of her warmed his heart. Would she consent to share his life? It was too soon to ask, but he knew he wouldn't be able to wait much longer.

Picking up a basket, Leah said, "I brought more decorations. These are the ones the children made at school."

For the next half hour, they hung slices of oranges and apples around the tree, along with pinecones that had been smeared with peanut butter and rolled in birdseed. The brightly colored yarn would supply the birds with soft nesting material come spring. When Joy couldn't reach the higher branches, Caleb lifted her and held her as Leah handed her more decorations. When they were finished, he put Joy down and she stood back. "Where's the star?"

"I have it right here." Leah produced a large gingerbread cookie shaped like a star and frosted white. She handed it to Caleb. He raised one eyebrow. "It's a little worldly for the birds, isn't it?"

"I think it's nearly perfect."

He propped the cookie in the upper branches and took a step away. Joy, her cheeks red from the cold, turned to Leah. "Can I show it to Pickles? She's never seen a Christmas tree."

"When she's a little older. Her eyes are open now. You must come and visit her soon."

"Can I, Daddy?"

"How about going there tonight?"

"Yeah!" She threw her arms around his legs. "This is the best surprise I ever had."

Emotion choked off Caleb's voice. What a true blessing this child was. If she had to go back to Valerie, he didn't know how he would face it.

"You are going to make many, many birds happy with your Christmas gift to them," Leah said.

Caleb cleared his throat. "Are you ready for another surprise?"

"Yes!" She jumped as she shouted.

He pointed toward the lane. "Go right through there. *Mammi* and *Daadi* are waiting for you."

As Joy took off, he turned to Leah and moved to stand directly in front of her. "Thank you for making my child so happy," he said softly.

"It was a joint effort." Leah's heart fluttered wildly. She had waited for days to be alone with him. They didn't have much time. People were expecting them. Would he kiss her again? Should she let him?

"It means a lot to me the way you've taken Joy under your wing. I was wondering…" He gazed into her eyes.

"Wondering what?" She licked her suddenly dry lips.

"I was wondering if I could kiss you again."

Chapter Fourteen

Caleb didn't wait for Leah's answer. She didn't have one anyway. He closed the space between them, wrapped his arms around her and pressed his mouth to hers. Leah closed her eyes to savor the tender excitement that made her slip her arms around his neck and pull him closer still.

His kiss, tender and tentative at first, deepened at her response. His firm lips drew forth an ardent desire that left her breathless and yet wanting more. When he pulled away, she was reluctant to let him go.

He raised his face to the sky as he drew a shuddering breath, then he cupped her head and pressed her face against his neck. He smelled like pine needles and the crisp outdoors, yet underneath it all was a wonderful earthiness that was uniquely his own scent.

He said, "I wish Christmas was over."

"Why?"

"Because then my parents wouldn't be waiting for us to join them and I could keep you to myself for a lot longer."

She gave a sigh of her own and stepped away. He released her, letting his hands slide down her arms slowly, as if he couldn't bear to let her go.

She had to know for certain what his intentions were

before she could let things go any further. "Caleb, does this mean you are staying? That you will become Amish?"

"Yes. I've thought about it and prayed about it. This is right for me. I know it."

Tears blurred her vision. "I'm so glad."

"Hey, don't cry."

"They are tears of happiness. You promised Joy she could visit the puppies. I see no reason why the two of you can't come over whenever you'd like."

He chuckled. "Don't give me an open invitation. I'll be outside your door every day when you get home from school."

"And what makes you think I would object to that?" She gave him a saucy smile and began walking toward the lane.

He quickly caught up with her. When they came out of the woods, she saw his parents were waiting for them in the sleigh. The big draft horse stomped one foot and shook his head, making the bells on his harness jingle.

Joy was already in the front seat between Maggie and Ike. "We're going for a sleigh ride. We're going to sing songs for our neighbors. And then go to town to see all the pretty lights."

Caleb spoke softly in Leah's ear. "Looks like we get the backseat to ourselves."

She quickly became the prim schoolteacher. "Where you will behave yourself, Caleb Mast. Or else."

"Or else what?" He helped her into the sleigh.

"Or else you will find yourself walking home. Ike, I think everyone should be at my place by now."

"We'll be there in two shakes of a lamb's tail. I reckon it's time I met this puppy I have heard so much about."

"You will love her," Joy assured him.

When they pulled into Leah's yard about twenty minutes later, they found four sleighs gathered there. Ike helped

Joy down from the seat. When they entered the house, she stopped. "What are all these people doing here?"

Leah said, "We are going caroling. Won't that be fun?"

Elam Sutter and his wife, Katie, along with their children, had arrived. Marvin Chupp sat at the kitchen table, with his cast stretched out in front of him and his crutches at his side. His wife stood behind him with her hands on his shoulders. Levi Beachy and Sarah each held a cup of the spiced cider that Leah had left simmering on the stove for everyone to enjoy. Levi's lanky twin teenage brothers flanked them. Jonathan and Karen Dresher were seated on the sofa with Nettie and Eli. The rest of the children were gathered around Trixie and her puppies. Leah was happy to see David in the group.

She looked around. "Are Wayne and Rhonda here?"

Sarah shook her head. "Wayne brought David, but he couldn't stay."

Leah tempered her disappointment with the knowledge that it was a small step for Wayne to allow David to join Caleb and Joy on the outing. She wondered if Rhonda knew that Caleb would be joining them.

"*Daadi,* come meet Pickles." Joy led the way to the box in the corner of the kitchen. The children gathered around it made room for them.

Joy greeted her friends. "Hi, Anna. Hi, Emmy. This is my grandpa. And this is Pickles." She carefully lifted the puppy from the box.

Ike admired Pickles and agreed that she looked like a very good farm dog in the making.

Leah said, "I think we are ready. Where shall we go first?"

Elam Sutter rose from his seat. "I know my neighbors the Zimmermans always enjoy hearing the children sing."

"So do Mr. and Mrs. McGregor," Katie added. "If we

make a loop around Pleasant View Road, we will end up in Hope Springs and we can give them a surprise concert."

With the route agreed upon, everyone went outside. Jonathan helped his pregnant wife into the backseat of Eli's sleigh. "This reminds me of the first time I rode in a sleigh with you, Karen. We were on our way to the Christmas program at Leah's school."

"I remember," Anna said. "You kissed my sister that night."

Karen frowned at her in surprise. "And how would you know that?"

"Jonathan told me that was the night he fell in love with you."

Karen tried to scowl at Jonathan, but she couldn't keep the smile off her face. "Should I know what else you have told my little sister about us?"

"Nope. Are you warm enough?"

"I will be when you get in."

Caleb spoke to Leah. "Will you ride with us?"

"Of course."

Jonathan called out, "Be careful, Caleb. Look what happened to me after one sleigh ride with the pretty Amish *maedel.*"

Leah blushed. "Ignore him," Karen said. "I do. You're in for a delightful night, Leah. Enjoy it."

Eli slapped the reins against his horse and drove out of the yard with Karen and Jonathan laughing together. Leah smiled at Caleb and got into the sleigh with happy anticipation coursing through her veins.

Maggie said, "It is hard to imagine that Jonathan was once an *Englisch* fellow. He is so at home with us. Caleb and Leah, get in so we can get going. This little girl wants to do some singing."

Caleb joined Leah in the backseat of the sleigh. He carefully tucked a blanket around them both. As Ike followed

the others out onto the road, Caleb realized that Karen was right. There was definitely something delightful about the night.

The fields they passed were blankets of white dotted with farmhouses and barns. The woods along the way were dark and gloomy. The light from the lanterns on the sides of the sleigh couldn't penetrate their depths. Overhead, the stars looked close enough to touch in the clear night air.

The cold stung his cheeks and made him wish he had a scarf to wrap around his face. The jingle of harness bells and the clip-clop of the horses' feet on the roadway were the only sounds. The glow of the lanterns on the other sleighs guided them forward.

Leah pulled the blanket higher. "I hope you didn't take offense at Jonathan's teasing."

"No. He is a good-natured fellow. I had forgotten how much fun it was to do simple things like this."

"I'm glad you have remembered."

In an hour's time, they visited four homes and stood in a semicircle around the children as they sang. Joy was off-key and a little slow, but her enthusiasm made up for her lack of talent. At each house, they were treated to baked goods and hot drinks before they climbed back in the sleighs and drove on.

They were nearing the end of Pleasant View Road when a dog darted out onto the road and began barking.

"Grandpa, stop. It's Duncan," Joy shouted.

Ike pulled over to the side. Duncan jumped into the sleigh and proceeded to lick Joy's face.

"*Ach,* get down, you silly mutt," Maggie scolded.

He scrambled off the seat and jumped down. Joy leaned over the side. "You need to come visit your babies. They need their daddy and their mommy."

He barked once and ran back the way he had come. Joy looked at Leah. "Is this where he lives?"

"*Ja,* it is Woolly Joe's farm. Duncan's owner, Carl King, lives in the shepherd's hut just beyond the fence."

"You should tell him to bring Duncan to see Pickles."

"I will mention it to him as soon as I see him." Leah exchanged an amused glance with Caleb.

He lowered his voice and leaned close. Beneath the quilt that covered them, he threaded his fingers between hers and held her hand. "Joy is a little like her father. When she gets an idea in her head, it's hard to make her let go of it. Duncan had better get his tail over to your place and wish his puppies a merry Christmas."

"And what idea do you have that you can't let go of?"

"At the moment, the only thing I don't want to let go of is your hand."

It was a night that Caleb would never forget. As they returned to Leah's home, he saw the way his life could unfold in Hope Springs. He and Joy would always be surrounded by his family and friends. The simple things—prayer, hard work and the company of men and women who sought to put God first in their lives—would fill the void that existed in his heart. If that life included Leah, it wouldn't be merely plain—it would be priceless.

The depth and intensity of his feelings for this woman frightened him. He wanted it to be real. He thought he had been in love before, but those emotions were nothing compared to this need to have Leah be a part of his life.

He didn't want to mess this up.

He gave her fingers a squeeze and then let go of her hand. He wouldn't rush her. He wanted her to be as certain of her feelings as he was.

Now that he was home, they would have plenty of time to discover if they were right for each other. Even if they were meant to be together, one huge issue remained unsolved. Rhonda's accusation.

If Leah couldn't accept his word over her sister's, how

could he consider a life together? If she believed he was lying about something so important, would she ever be able to trust his word?

He glanced at the woman seated beside him. Somehow, he had to make her believe he wasn't David's father. He prayed God would show him how to do the impossible.

For Leah, the following week was a whirlwind of activity. There was so much to do to get her students ready for the Christmas pageant, make her own Christmas preparations and still maintain the class work the children needed. Each day, they practiced their songs and rehearsed their parts after school.

Joy blossomed when she learned she would be included in the school program. For the entire week, she worked so hard it was almost painful to watch, but each success made Joy that much more determined to master her part.

It wasn't until Friday evening that she and Caleb came over to visit the puppy. Joy proceeded to tell Leah that she didn't need her daddy to walk her to school anymore.

Leah glanced at Caleb, who was sitting at her kitchen table. He shrugged. "I told her I didn't think it was a good idea for her to go by herself."

"I'm not going by myself. David is gonna walk with me. He is gonna walk to Grandma and Grandpa's house, and then we are gonna go to school together just like you and your brother did when you were little."

"That sounds like a very good plan," Leah said.

Caleb slowly shook his head. "I don't think so."

"It will make David walk an extra quarter of a mile each day both to and from school, but if he wants to do it, I don't see why you should object. He does walk over to visit your parents on his own."

"He's only nine years old."

"He is a levelheaded boy. You roamed the countryside

when you were his age. No one gave it a second thought. It's nice that he and Joy can be friends and playmates. It will be good for both of them. For the whole family."

Joy folded her hands together. "Please, Daddy, I want to walk with David. He's my real friend."

He hesitated. Leah gave him a sympathetic smile. "You can always follow behind them and make sure they get where they're going."

His sheepish grin told her that was exactly what he had been thinking. "All right, you can walk with David. If it's okay with his parents."

"Cool." Joy returned to playing with the puppies. They were getting big enough to waddle around outside their box. Joy giggled as all three of them tried to climb into her lap.

Leah took a seat across from Caleb at the table. "She will grow up no matter how hard you try to prevent it."

"You're right, but I'm not ready for it."

"How is your job search going?"

"Not well. I'm tired of freeloading off my parents."

"I'm sure they don't consider it freeloading. I know you help your father with his chores."

"Sure, but it's nothing that he can't do himself."

Suddenly, she heard a buzzing noise. Caleb reached into his pocket and pulled out his cell phone. She was disappointed that he hadn't given up all of his worldly things.

He folded it shut and put it back in his pocket without answering it. "I'll let it go to voice mail. It's my old boss. I'd like to get rid of the phone, but my attorney says I need to be easily accessible until the custody issue is resolved."

She glanced at Joy to see if the child was listening. Assured that her attention was on the puppies, Leah asked, "Have you heard anything new?"

"They are still trying to locate Valerie. She can fight it if she wants."

Leah watched Joy putting the puppies back inside the

box. "If she knew how happy Joy was now, I think she would agree that you have done the right thing."

Joy came to stand beside them. "Has Duncan been here to visit?"

Leah shook her head. "If he has, I haven't seen him."

Joy propped her hands on her hips. "That dog is a dead-beat dad. I'm gonna have a talk with him."

Leah and Caleb exchanged an amused glance as they struggled not to laugh.

He stood and said, "We should be getting home, Joy. Thank Leah for letting you visit with Pickles, Peanut Butter and Jelly."

"I enjoy watching her as much as she enjoys playing with them. I'm sorry I've been so busy that you had to wait until now." It had been almost a week since the caroling party. Nearly a whole week since the last time he had kissed her.

Caleb smiled in understanding. "After Christmas, we will all have more time to spend together."

"I look forward to that," she said with a tender smile.

Joy pulled on her coat. "*Danki,* Leah. See you at school. Our program is three days away, and Christmas is the day after that and it's my birthday, too. I'm gonna have so much fun. Come on, Daddy, we have to check my Christmas tree on the way home. Those birds are eating everything."

She charged out the door, leaving Caleb and Leah alone for a moment. He crossed the room and gave her a quick kiss. "Until after Christmas."

She closed the door behind them and leaned against it. It was all happening so fast. Only a month ago, she had been horrified to see him return to Hope Springs. Now she never wanted him or his daughter to leave.

It was snowing again. Large light flakes floated down like feathers. Caleb listened to the message from his former boss on the walk home. "Mast, I know you're still vis-

iting your family in Ohio, but if you want that transfer to Brazil, we got an opening. I can't hold it for long so let me know soon as you can."

Caleb closed his phone and put it in his pocket. A month ago, he would've jumped at the chance to rake in a bigger salary and see a bit of the world. None of it seemed important now. He glanced at his daughter. She had changed everything.

His phone rang again. Caleb already knew what he would say when he talked to his boss. He opened the phone, but the name on the screen wasn't Sanford Limited. It was his attorney. He pressed the button to talk. "This is Caleb."

"Mr. Mast, I'm glad I reached you. We found her."

Caleb stopped walking. "And?"

"She relinquished all rights. You have sole and permanent custody of your daughter. Congratulations. We'll get you copies of the paperwork as soon as we can."

Caleb didn't hear anything else his attorney said. His relief was overwhelming. He bent forward and braced his hand on his knee. He never had to worry about losing Joy again. Until this moment, he hadn't realized how heavy that worry had been. He felt as if he could float up off the earth.

He walked back to the house with Joy and marveled at the journey the Lord had taken them on. At the front steps, he said, "Go on in and tell my folks I have something I need to do. I'll be home later." Once Joy was inside, Caleb turned and jogged toward Leah's house. He needed to share this with her as soon as possible.

Leah was surprised when Trixie alerted her to another visitor. She looked out her window and saw Caleb standing just off her porch. Why had he come back so soon? Snowflakes swirled around him. He had his hands in his pockets. He looked uncertain and alone.

She happily opened the door. "You should come in before you turn into a snowman."

He managed a smile. "It is a little cold out here."

She stepped aside and let him in. Her foolish heart was about to jump out of her chest. "Would you like some coffee?"

"That would be great."

She set about filling the pot with fresh water and spooning the grounds into the basket. "Did you forget something?"

"No."

"Joy is so excited about Christmas."

"Joy is the reason I'm here. No, that's not exactly true. I'm here because of you."

She wiped her hands on her apron. Suddenly he crossed the room and grasped her hands. Startled, she stared into his eyes. They were dark with emotion. "When I first arrived, I never planned to stay here, but from the moment we met, I haven't been able to stop thinking about you."

"Nor I about you."

"I'm not very good at this. I know this is too soon, but I want you to know that I have fallen in love with you, Leah Belier. I never intended to. I tried not to, but you are an overwhelming force of nature."

"I'm not sure whether to be flattered or not."

"I just learned that Valerie has relinquished all rights to Joy. She and I are free to stay here."

"How sad for her, but how wonderful for you."

"There is something I have to ask you."

She laid a hand on his lips. "Before you say anything, I must speak. I have forgiven you for everything in the past. It took me a long time to let go of my anger, but you have made me see that people really can change."

He smiled sadly. "In all the years I was gone, I never belonged anywhere. I blamed that on the events of my life.

I tried to find a place where I could be happy, but I always came up short. Until I came home. I want to stay now. I want you to want me to stay."

"I do. Caleb, you and Joy have come to mean so much to me. I can't imagine my life without you. You have my forgiveness. We will never mention the past again."

He caressed her cheek with the back of his knuckles. "I treasure the fact that you forgive me, but I'm not the father of your sister's child."

She turned her face away from his touch. "Caleb, please."

He took a step away from her. "I wanted everyone to know the truth. I wanted to hold my head up. Most of all I wanted my family to believe me. It doesn't matter anymore what other people think, but I need to hear it from you. I need to hear that *you* believe me."

"Caleb, you're asking me to call my sister a liar."

"Yes, I am."

Leah pressed a hand to her forehead. This was her worst nightmare. "Don't do this. Don't make me choose."

The light went out of his eyes. Grayness settled over his face. "I guess that's my answer, then, isn't it?" He turned toward the door.

"Caleb, wait."

He paused with his hand on the door, but he didn't look at her. "Wait for what, Leah? What will change your mind? A DNA test? Rhonda won't consent to that because she knows I'm not the father. I asked you for too much. I'm sorry. How can there be anything between us if you think I'm a heartless liar?"

She crossed the room to lay her hands on his arm. "I want to believe you, Caleb. I want to believe my sister, too. All I can do is say the past is the past. I know you aren't like that now. You're a fine, caring man and a good father."

"Maybe it's in the past for you, but not for me." He opened the door and walked out.

Leah put a hand behind her to search for the table, and staggered on trembling legs until she ran into it. She didn't have the strength to stand up. She collapsed onto a chair and put her head in her hands. How could such a wonderful night have turned out so horribly wrong?

"Oh, Caleb, what have we done?" She buried her face in her arms and wept.

Caleb wiped the tears from his cheeks before he entered the house. Thankfully, his parents had already gone to bed. He climbed the steps to his room and paused at Joy's door to check in on her. She was sleeping peacefully. His tears started flowing again.

He shut her door, sat on the edge of his bed and tried to figure out what to do now. Now that his precious dream had crumbled to dust. He couldn't blame Leah for supporting her sister. The fact that Wayne hadn't believed his side of the story had cut like a knife.

At least Joy was safe and happy now. That part of his plan had worked out. He lay back and covered his eyes with his arm. Where did he go from here?

He didn't get much sleep, but he eventually came to a decision. When he heard his parents stirring downstairs the next morning, he rose and went down, too. His mother took one look at his face and knew something was wrong.

"Caleb, what is it?" She clutched her apron in her hands.

He tried to smile and allay her worry. "I had a call from my attorney yesterday."

"It's bad news?"

"No, it's good news. Valerie has relinquished her rights. Joy will be able to stay here forever."

"It is sad for the child's mother but *wunderbaar* for us." His mother turned back to the stove.

Caleb's father read between the lines. "Joy will stay with us, but you will not."

His mother spun around. "Why do you say that?"

"I have to go back to Texas for a while. There is paperwork that needs to be done. I have my place to put on the market. It may take a few months, so I'll be taking a job down there."

"Months? So long?" She glanced at her husband.

Ike drew a deep breath. "We will take *goot* care of Joy until you return."

"I knew you would."

"Where are you going, Daddy?" Joy stood in the doorway with a look of panic on her face.

He forced a bright smile. "Good morning, kiddo. Come here, I have something to tell you."

She crossed the room slowly. He sat in a chair and lifted her onto his lap. "Do you remember when I said I would never leave without telling you where I'm going and when I'll be back?"

"Yes."

"Joy, I have to go to Texas for a while. You know I've been looking for a job and I can't find one here, but I have a job waiting for me in Houston. I'll need to stay there for several months, so I can't tell you exactly when I'll be back."

He wasn't lying. He would be back. To visit, but not to stay and build a life as he once thought. He couldn't bear facing Leah time and again, knowing his love for her was hopeless.

"When are you going?"

"Tomorrow."

His mother started sniffling and left the room.

Tears formed in Joy's eyes. "But you will miss my program and my birthday."

He hated to disappoint her, but wasn't it better to make a quick clean break? She would be so busy she wouldn't even miss him, but he was going to miss her.

It wasn't for her sake that he was leaving so soon. He

was a coward. He couldn't bear to drag out the parting. He couldn't stand to face Leah again knowing how much he loved her and knowing she would never believe his side of the story.

"I'm sorry about that, but you can tell me all about your program and Christmas when we talk. Grandpa will take you to use the phone at the neighbor's house so we can stay in touch. You can call me anytime. He and Grandma will be there for your program, so you won't be alone. Okay?"

"I guess." She got off his lap and left the room.

His father said, "Caleb, you are making a big mistake."

"Mistakes are what I seem to do best, Dad." He rose and went to his room to pack.

Chapter Fifteen

Leah didn't leave her house on Saturday. All she did was cry and ask God why He had allowed her to fall in love with someone who broke her heart. If she indulged in self-pity, there was no one but Trixie to see. No one to tell her she was better off without Caleb. No one who could lend her a shoulder to cry on. She was a foolish spinster who lived with a dog. If she had been content with her lot, she wouldn't be grieving now.

It wasn't until Sunday evening that she finally got a grip on her tattered emotions. She began to analyze her last conversation with Caleb without the hurt and anger clouding her judgment.

Caleb had asked her to believe he wasn't David's father. After years of thinking that was the case, she repeated what she believed was true. Rhonda said he was the father. Rhonda wouldn't lie.

Or would she?

Caleb had been sincere. He desperately wanted Leah to believe him even if she was the only one who did. It would have been much easier for him to accept her forgiveness and let it go at that. They could have been happy together, for she'd meant it when she said she forgave him. She never

would have mentioned it again. Had he cast her aside out of false pride?

He'd said he loved her. She believed that. If she loved him, and God help her, she did, then she had to believe in him. Caleb was telling the truth.

So why had Rhonda lied?

It was time to find out. Leah wouldn't leave her sister's house until everything was out in the open.

It was late by the time Leah drove up and stopped in front of her sister's gate, but there was a single lamp burning in the kitchen. Through the window, she could see Rhonda scrubbing the kitchen floor, always the last chore of her day. She looked up in surprise when Leah walked in.

"Sister, what are you doing here? Is something wrong?"

"Where's Wayne?"

Rhonda propped her mop against the wall. "He's out in the barn. One of the horses has foundered. What's going on?"

"Where is David?"

"He's outside with Wayne. Are you going to tell me what you're doing here?"

"You lied about Caleb being the father of your child. Why?"

Leah waited for her sister's reply. She couldn't believe she was questioning her sister's honesty, but either Caleb was lying or her sister was. In her heart, Leah wanted to believe both spoke the truth, but that wasn't possible.

Rhonda turned away. "How can you say such a thing? Do you think I would lie about something like that?"

The hesitation in her sister's voice told Leah the truth. Her legs buckled. She sat down at the kitchen table. "Oh, Rhonda, why did you do it?"

If only she'd had the courage to believe Caleb. Would he forgive her for doubting her?

Rhonda spun back, her eyes snapping with anger. "How can you believe that outsider over your own sister?"

"You ruined his life."

"He ruined my life. Look at my face."

"Who is David's father?"

"Caleb."

Anger gave Leah a strength she never suspected she possessed. Springing to her feet, she grabbed her sister's shoulders and shook her. "Do you even know how to tell the truth?"

Rhonda pushed her away and folded her arms tightly across her chest. She seemed to shrink into herself. "Why can't you leave it be?"

"Because I'm in love with Caleb and because I don't want to see you suffering anymore. Tell me what happened. Please, Rhonda."

"It isn't a pretty tale."

When they sat beside each other on the sofa, Rhonda said, "I didn't blame Caleb for what happened. It was an accident. I knew that. He tried so hard to make it up to me. He took me home from church a few times. He talked me into going to a singing, but I was self-conscious, I didn't like people staring at me."

"So when did you meet David's father?"

A look of disgust flooded Rhonda's eyes. "He came to our house. You remember him. He took me to the police station to make a statement about the accident."

"Drake Colburn? An *Englisch* officer of the law?" She hadn't expected that.

"At first, he was nice to me. He made me feel pretty again. I thought I was in love with him. I even considered running away to be with him. Then I found out he was married. He was only using me. I was such a fool."

"Oh, Rhonda, I'm so sorry you went through that. Did Drake know you were pregnant?"

Rhonda's eyes widened. "He doesn't know David is his. He can't know. Don't you see? David is proof of what he did. He could take my son away. He has the English law on his side. His wife was never able to have children."

"Rhonda, I don't believe he could take David from you."

"I can't risk it. Don't you see that?" She choked back a sob.

"Why say Caleb was the father? Was it because you blamed him for what had happened to you?"

"I thought if I told Caleb what had happened that he would marry me and make everything right. He had been so kind."

"So Caleb knew?"

"*Nee,* I had so much morning sickness that *Mamm* guessed what was wrong before I had a chance to tell Caleb. She and *Daed* confronted me. I panicked. I told them Caleb was the father. I was too ashamed to admit what had really happened. *Daed* was so angry. He made me go with him to see Caleb's parents that day and demand that he do the right thing."

"But Caleb wouldn't."

"When he denied it, I didn't know what to say. Once I accused him of being the father, I couldn't change my story. I surely couldn't tell *Daed* and *Mamm* the truth. I never expected Caleb to leave. I honestly thought that he would come around and accept that he had to marry me."

"No one believed him, and everyone believed you." Her sister had suffered a great wrong, but Caleb was a victim, too.

"When Wayne offered to marry me, I thought my nightmare was finally over. I knew I was breaking your heart, but you are so pretty, and you are so smart, I thought you would find someone else to love. Can you forgive me?"

"Wayne wasn't the one for me. I know that now. Does Wayne know about Drake?"

Rhonda clutched Leah's arm. "Wayne gave you up, he disowned his brother, all because of my lie. How could I tell him it was all for nothing? You can't tell him. Promise me you won't tell him. I couldn't bear to see him look at me with more contempt than he already does."

"It's none of my business, but it's clear that things aren't right between the two of you."

Rhonda pressed a hand to her cheek. "He can't stand to look at my face. He thinks I'm hideous."

Neither of them had heard Wayne enter the house until he spoke. "I don't find you hideous. It is my own guilt I can't abide when I look at you."

Startled, they both faced him. There were tears on his face.

"You heard!" Rhonda wailed. She sank to the floor and covered her face with her hands.

He crossed the room, ignoring Leah, and dropped to his knees in front of his wife. "I heard, and I would give anything to undo the pain you suffered. You are not hideous. Your face is beautiful to me."

"But I lied to you."

"I, too, have lived a lie, *mein lieb,* my own true love. I was the one driving the car the night of your accident. I thought I killed you. I ran home and Caleb found me cowering in the barn. I was so frightened I couldn't move. He raced to your side. He got help and saved your life."

Leah shook her head. "But Caleb took the blame for the whole thing."

Wayne looked up at her. "I tried to tell my father it was my fault, but the words stuck in my throat. I couldn't bear for him to know of my shame. Caleb was always in trouble. It was easy for everyone to believe he'd done such a reckless thing. My father shunned him. As the days went on, I grew terrified that Caleb would reveal the truth about that night. That's why I was glad he left and why I wanted

him to leave again. I'm ashamed of what I have become. Rhonda, can you forgive me?"

"Now you know David has an English father, you must hate me."

He took her hands between his. "David is my son in every way. I could not love him more if I tried. Please believe that."

She gazed into his eyes. "I do. I pray you will someday love me, too."

He gently pressed a hand to her scarred cheek. "We have much to learn about each other now that there are no more secrets between us. If it takes me a lifetime, I will earn your love."

"It won't take that long, for you already have my heart."

He cupped her face and kissed her.

Leah left them alone and walked into the kitchen. She made coffee because she needed to do something. All Caleb had asked of her was to have faith in him, to trust him, and she had turned him away. She would tell him how wrong she had been and beg his forgiveness.

The outside door opened, startling her. Ike Mast came in, shaking the snow from his hat. He searched the room with his eyes and then focused on Wayne and Rhonda. "Is Joy here with you?"

Leah stared at him in shock. "No. How long has she been missing?"

"Maybe an hour. I'm not sure. She went to her room after supper. When I checked on her before I turned in, she was gone."

"Have you been to my house? She loves to visit the puppies."

"I came here first. I think she is upset because Caleb is gone."

Disbelief stole Leah's voice. A loud buzzing filled her head. No. Had she driven him away with her doubts? What

had she done? Rhonda came to her side and put her arms around her. Leah leaned against her, thankful for her support.

Wayne stared at his father. "What do you mean, Caleb is gone?"

"He left two hours ago to drive back to Texas. I don't know why. I thought he had found peace with us."

Caleb paced the small confines of a service station waiting room just off Interstate 77. He had been on the road for only twenty minutes when his check-engine light came on. At least he'd caught a break when he found a place open on Sunday. Outside, the snow was picking up. He wanted to get on the road. The last place he wanted to be was stuck in Ohio in a snowstorm.

He carried his foam cup of lousy coffee to the window. Half the parking lot was blocked off by sawhorses with yellow flashing lights on top and *caution* written in black letters across them.

A fellow traveler came through the door. He stamped his feet on the worn rug. "Do you work here?"

Caleb shook his head. "I'm just waiting to find out how much it is going to cost me to drive out of here."

The shop owner came in from the service bay, wiping his hands on a pink rag. He patted his salt-and-pepper hair into place, scratched his grizzled whiskers and finished wiping his hands on his stained overalls. "What can I do for you, sir?"

"I think I made a wrong turn. Do you have a map?"

Caleb turned back to stare at the flashing caution lights outside. He saw the reflection of the two men behind him as they leaned over the map. The store owner jabbed a finger at the paper. "This is where you made your mistake."

Caleb heard the echo of his father's voice. *Caleb, you are making a mistake.*

The traveler leaned forward to examine the map more closely. "So how do I get on the right road?"

Outside the caution lights continued to blink their warning. *Don't come this way.* Which way should he go? Caleb closed his eyes. *Which way, God?*

The shop owner said, "It's not easy to get there from here. You're going to have to go back a ways."

"I hate making mistakes. This is costing me so much time."

Mistakes are what I seem to do best, Dad. Caleb opened his eyes. If he knew it was a mistake, why was he leaving?

The shop owner took a pen and marked something on the map, then he pushed it toward his customer. "Jumping out of an airplane without a parachute is a mistake you can't fix. Most everything else just takes a little more effort to make it right. Go back about ten miles and follow this road. It will take you where you need to be."

The traveler thanked him and left. The shop owner looked at Caleb. "Mr. Mast, your truck is done. It was just a loose wire. I'm not even going to charge you for the time it took me to fix it." He held out the keys.

Caleb took them and stared at the Texas emblem on his key chain. What was there in Texas for him really? Nothing as important as the people he'd left behind. He would find a job. He would beg Leah to marry him, and if she didn't, he would still raise his beautiful daughter, as a good Amish father should.

"Where are you headed, son?" the man asked with a gap-toothed smile.

Caleb grinned, tossed the keys in the air and caught them again. "Home. I'm headed home. I just didn't know it until now."

Wayne quickly took charge. "We'll start a search for Joy. It's not a night for a child to be wandering around the

countryside. Leah, go to your house. Take David with you. If Joy isn't there, send David with a message to Eli Imhoff to meet us at *Daed*'s house. He'll send word for more men. I'll saddle David's pony and tie him behind your buggy."

"Where is David?" Rhonda asked.

"He came back to the house some time ago," Wayne replied.

Rhonda looked surprised. "I didn't see him come in. I'll check his room." She hurried away.

Leah looked at the men. "We should get a message to Caleb."

Ike nodded in agreement. "If Joy isn't at your house, stop at our neighbor's farm and use their phone. Caleb left us his cell phone number." He handed her a card.

Leah took it and tucked it in her pocket. She quickly pulled on her coat and tied her bonnet under her chin. "Don't worry, Ike. I'm sure she is with my puppies."

Rhonda burst back into the room, her eyes wide with panic. "David isn't in his room. He never leaves without telling me where he's going. Where could he be?"

Leah could think of only one thing that made sense. "He must be with Joy."

Wayne drew his frightened wife into his arms. "David is a smart and resourceful boy. He will take good care of Joy if they are together."

Leah said, "Wayne, come with me. Rhonda, stay here in case they come back. Ike, I think you should go home. I know Maggie must be out of her mind with worry. If they have returned, you can bring word to Rhonda. We'll coordinate the search from here."

Leah prayed for the safety of the children as she and Wayne scrambled into her buggy. Ten minutes later, she pulled up in front of her own house. The windows were dark.

"Joy, are you in here? David?" She rushed through the

front door and nearly tripped over Trixie. The dog ran outside, barking furiously.

Wayne came in behind Leah. "Are they here?"

"Nee."

Trixie stood on the front porch, barking into the night. Something was wrong. Leah lit the lamp she kept by the front door. The soft glow illuminated the empty kitchen.

"I will check the barn," Wayne said.

As he went out the door, Trixie came back in and went to her box. She whined as she nosed her litter. Leah quickly checked the rest of the house. She came back to the kitchen just as Wayne returned. She looked at him hopefully. "Anything?"

"Nee. The snow is coming down hard now."

"Do you think they might have gone to the school?"

Trixie barked sharply. Wayne glanced her way. "What's wrong with your dog?"

"I don't know. She's not usually like this." Leah crossed the room. She held the lamp over the whelping box. Only two puppies were snuggled together in the corner. "Pickles is missing."

She quickly checked the room, but Trixie's behavior told her the puppy wasn't close by. "I think the children took the puppy with them."

"At least we know that they came this way. You go to Eli's place and send the others here."

She blinked back tears. "It will take so long to gather everyone."

"Have faith, Leah. Our children are in God's hands. They always have been."

As they started out the door, the lights of an English car turned into the yard. Leah thought Ike must have gone to the English farm and called for help. Now they could gather the neighbors quickly and begin the search.

She realized almost immediately that it wasn't a car. It

was a pickup. The same kind of pickup that Caleb drove. The truck stopped. Her knees almost buckled when she saw him get out.

"Thank You, God, for bringing him back." She flew into his arms.

He held her tight. "Your forgiveness is enough. I will never ask for more. I can't face a life without you and my daughter in it. I can't."

"I love you, Caleb. I know the truth. I'm so sorry that I doubted you, but darling, Joy is missing. She and David have run away."

Caleb's mind went numb with shock. "How long has she been gone? Is anyone looking for her?"

Wayne approached them. "It's good to see you, brother. We think they've been gone about two hours now. We are getting up a search party. Can you drive us to alert our neighbors?"

"Of course. Get in. Where were they last seen?" Caleb held open the door as Leah climbed in. Wayne quickly went around to the passenger side.

"We know that they came here and took one of Leah's puppies with them. Do you have any idea where Joy would go?"

The instant Wayne shut his door, Caleb stepped on the gas. "The Christmas tree. We should check there. She wanted to show the puppy her tree."

The truck fishtailed briefly in the snow. Caleb slowed down. He couldn't find his daughter if he wound up in the ditch. "I never should've left. This is my fault."

If anything happened to Joy or to David, he would never forgive himself.

It took only a few minutes to reach the place close to Joy's tree. Caleb parked on the side of the lane and

raced into the woods, calling her name. Only silence answered him.

Leah and Wayne joined him. Wayne held a flashlight he had taken from Caleb's glove box. He scanned the ground. "I don't see any fresh tracks in the snow. I don't think they have been here."

"Now what?" Leah looked to both of them.

Caleb raked a hand through his hair. He'd never been more frightened in his life. Wayne laid a hand on his shoulder. "We should let our folks know you have returned. The children may already be there."

Caleb nodded. If they weren't, he would gather men to help him search if he had to drive to every farm in the valley.

They returned to the truck and drove to the house. His parents hurried out to meet them. Caleb could see by their faces that the children weren't there. His mother threw her arms around him and held on tight without saying a word.

He gently pulled her arms down and held her hands. "We'll find them."

"I know you will."

The sound of muffled hoof beats reached Caleb. He turned to see a horse and cart coming into the yard. A burly man in a knitted cap and long coat got down and lifted a bundle of blankets from the backseat. David climbed down from behind him. Caleb's heart stopped beating.

Leah said, "It's Carl King."

Maggie and Wayne rushed to embrace David. Carl nodded to Caleb. "Are you missing a couple of naughty children?"

"We are," Caleb managed to say past the lump in his throat.

Carl handed his bundle to Caleb. He pulled back the edge of the blanket. Joy's eyes fluttered open. "I fell asleep."

Her eyes opened wide and then scrunched with happiness as she grinned at him. "Daddy, is that you?"

He sat down in the snow and held her tight. "It's me, baby."

"You're squishing me, again."

"Too bad. You will get squished a lot from now on. Get used to it." *Thank You, dear Lord, for delivering her safely into my arms. Thank You so much.*

Carl shoved his hands in his coat pockets. "She came to scold my dog for not visiting his puppies. Called him a deadbeat dad. You're gonna have your hands full with that one, Caleb Mast."

Joy wiggled until she had her head free. "Where is Pickles?"

Carl went back to the cart and produced the puppy from a basket under the seat. He handed her to Joy, who held her close.

"*Danki,* Mr. King."

"*Du bischt wilkumm.*" He walked back toward his cart.

Caleb handed Joy to his father and went after Carl. He held out his hand. "Thank you."

Carl looked at Caleb's hand and then at his face. Quietly, he asked, "Are you a baptized member of the Amish?"

"I will be soon."

"After that, you cannot shake my hand."

That meant Carl had been excommunicated by his congregation. He was under the *Meidung,* shunned. Caleb kept his hand outstretched. "Then I need to thank you now."

Carl shook Caleb's hand. He got in his cart and drove away into the swirling snow. Caleb wondered briefly what mistake had driven the man into such a position. He turned back to where his family and Leah were gathered. He had his own mistakes to right.

It was after midnight before Wayne and Rhonda gathered their sleepy son from Caleb's room and took him

home. Earlier, David told them he had been on his way to the house when he spotted Joy walking alone through the woods. He went after her but couldn't convince her to return home, so he went along with her to make sure she was safe.

Leah waved to her sister and Wayne as they left, and returned to the living room, where Caleb stood by the fireplace. His parents had gone to bed an hour before.

Caleb held out his arms. "Come here."

She snuggled up beside him. He draped an arm around her shoulder and pulled her close. It wasn't proper behavior for a schoolteacher, but Leah didn't care. There was nowhere in the world she would rather be and no one she would rather be with.

"It has been quite a night," he said and kissed the top of her head.

"Now that everyone's story is out in the open, I know the healing will start."

He lifted her face so that he could look into her eyes. "God did a wondrous thing when He brought me back to you and to my faith. I plan to be baptized as soon as possible so that I may experience all of His grace in this life and in the next."

"I'm so glad. I know this is what He wants for you."

"Have I told you how much I love you?"

"You have told me a little, but I don't think you told me enough. You might have to write it on the blackboard one hundred times."

He laughed. "What if I give you one hundred kisses instead?"

She pretended to think it over. "That will be acceptable."

His lips met hers and he proceeded to make her forget everything that had once stood between them. It lasted long enough to leave her breathless and hungry for more. He drew away slightly. "One."

"I'm ready for two."

"So am I, but I have one question to ask you first."

"What is that?"

"Will you marry me?"

"I should hold out until at least kiss five or kiss six."

"You do know how to torture a man. Okay."

He cupped her face in his hands and gave her five quick pecks on her cheek. "What is your answer?"

She moved away and folded her arms. "I've forgotten the question."

"Leah, you make my heart sing. You are going to be a wonderful mother for Joy."

"I can't wait for the day." It was the truth. She was about to have a special child, a special gift, courtesy of God and Caleb Mast.

He moved close and brushed his fingers along the edge of her *kapp*. "I can't wait for the day that I will see you with your hair down. You are so beautiful."

She trembled at the thought of what marriage to him would mean. "You're getting ahead of yourself. I haven't said yes."

"You have hit your limit of six kisses. Not another one until you say you will marry me."

She cupped his face between her hands. "You drive a hard bargain. Very well, I will gladly marry you."

His next kiss lasted longer than the first. A small voice that broke them apart. "You guys, I had a bad dream."

Leah tried to step away, but Caleb held on to her. "You have lousy timing, Joy, but come here and tell us all about your bad dream."

He moved to sit on the sofa and pulled Leah down beside him. Joy crossed the room and sat in between them. "I think it's gone. I don't remember what it was about."

Caleb brushed her hair away from her face. "In that case, I think you need to go back to bed. It's very late."

Joy tipped her head to the side and looked at him. "If you marry Leah, will that make her my *aenti?*"

He shared a sheepish grin with Leah. She said, "*Nee,* it will make me your new *mamm.* Will that be all right with you?"

"*Ja,* that will be *goot!*"

On Christmas Eve, Leah took the stage at the end of her students' final song. "And now we will have a play that isn't listed on your programs. This is a special presentation written and narrated by Anna Imhoff with Joy Perry Mast, David Mast, Kyle Troyer and Noah Imhoff as the players."

Anna walked out onstage. "A long time ago, in a land far away, there were shepherds tending their flocks in the hills near the little town of Bethlehem."

Leah stepped behind the curtain as David, Noah and Kyle walked on. They all carried shepherds crooks and wore long robes. They stopped and began to lay sticks together as if they were going to build a fire.

Kyle said, "Do you hear that? It sounds like singing."

"I don't hear anything. It's just the wind," David replied.

"And, lo, the angel of the Lord came upon them, and the glory of the Lord shone round about them. And they were sore afraid." Anna stepped away from the center of the stage.

Behind the curtain, Leah gave Joy a little push. "That's your cue."

Joy walked out to the middle of the stage. The paper wings pinned to the back of her white dress fluttered gently.

She paused and looked toward Leah. Leah nodded. "Go ahead."

Joy stood tall. "Fear not—for, behold, I bring you good tidings of great joy." She smiled at the audience. "My name is Joy."

Anna whispered, "Which shall be…"

Joy grew stern. "Which shall be to all people. For unto you is born this day in the city of David—"

She stopped and pointed at the shepherds kneeling before her. "This is my cousin. His name is David, too. For unto you is born this day in the city of David, a Savior, which is Christ the Lord. And this shall be a sign unto you. You can find him wrapped in swaddling clothes, lying in a manger. That's a cow feeder."

A ripple of suppressed laughter came from the audience. Anna stepped onstage again. "And suddenly there was with the angel a multitude of the heavenly host praising God, and saying…" She held her hand toward the children lined up along the wall.

They shouted as one. "Glory to God in the highest, and on earth peace, goodwill toward men."

Anna looked out over the audience. "And it came to pass, as the angels were gone away from them into heaven…"

"Oh, I have to leave." Joy waved at everyone and left the stage.

Anna composed herself. "The shepherds said one to another, Let us now go even unto Bethlehem, and see this thing which is come to pass, which the Lord hath made known unto us. And they came with haste, and found Mary, and Joseph, and the babe lying in a manger. And when they had seen it, they made known abroad the saying, which was told them concerning this child. And all they that heard it wondered at those things which were told them by the shepherds."

Anna held one hand high. "In this way, the good news of our salvation began to spread, thanks to the shepherds in the fields."

Joy rushed out onto the stage. "I have more good news. My daddy is going to stay here with me. He is going to marry my teacher, Leah. She's not going to be my teacher anymore. That makes me sad, but she is going to be my

mamm, and that makes me happy. Oh, and Pickles is gonna be our dog. *Frehlicher Grischtdaag,* everyone. That means Merry Christmas!"

Joy hurried off the stage to Leah's side. "How did I do?"

Leah caught Caleb's amused and loving smile from the audience. She put her arm around Joy and grinned at the child of her heart. "Darling, that was an unforgettable performance."

* * * * *

Dear Reader,

I hope you enjoyed Caleb, Leah and Joy's journey to discover Christmas in Amish country. You may have noticed that there was more than one love story developing throughout the book. One was Caleb's love for Leah. The other was Caleb's growing relationship with his newfound daughter, Joy.

Children with Down syndrome present a number of challenges to their parents, but they also bring great joy to those who know and love them. Caleb was shocked to learn he had a special-needs child, but in true hero fashion, he set about doing what he believed was best for his little girl, even if that meant a life without him. Thankfully, Leah entered the picture at just the right time to help him see what Joy needed was a father's unconditional love.

The Lord brings many challenges to our lives. Sometimes, it is impossible to understand the reason for the pain we endure, but the one thing we are never without is His unconditional love. He's beside us in every trial, even when we don't know it.

May the Lord bless and keep you this Christmas season and may He bring you and yours abundant joy. Be mindful of the true meaning of Christmas, and as the Amish do so beautifully, keep it in your heart, always.

Frehlicher Grischtdaag,
(And that means Merry Christmas.)

Patricia Davids

Questions for Discussion

1. Were you aware that the Amish consider special-needs children as special gifts from God? How do you think society in general views children with disabilities such as Down syndrome?

2. When Leah came face-to-face with Caleb after so many years, she realized she hadn't forgiven him for the damage he caused her family. Why is true forgiveness so hard to embrace?

3. Did any element of this story change your perception of the Amish faith? If so, what was that and why?

4. Amish schools resemble the public classrooms of a hundred years ago. My dad was the one who told me about playing Duck, Duck, Goose. What games do you remember playing on the school grounds when you were young?

5. What Christmas traditions do you enjoy in your home that would be acceptable in an Amish household?

6. My family has a Christmas season tradition of decorating our tree on my grandson's December 2 birthday. What Christmas traditions would you find hardest to leave behind if you were to become Amish?

7. What was your favorite scene in the story and why?

8. What was your least favorite scene in the story and why?

9. I vividly remember playing the part of Mary in our school Christmas pageant when I was ten. What are

some of your fond memories of school or church Christmas programs?

10. Amish schoolteachers are usually unmarried women with only an eighth-grade education themselves. Very rarely an Amish man may teach school. Do you feel this type of education system hinders or helps the Amish? Why?

11. Caleb thought the best place for Joy to grow up would be with his Amish parents. Why was he right in that assumption? Was he wrong?

12. Joy had a good time thinking up names for Leah's puppies. What are some unusual pet names that you've heard? For instance, my vet treats a cat named Two and a Half, and I once met a sled dog named Ford F-150.

13. Anna Imhoff is a character who first appeared in my book *An Amish Christmas*. How did Anna's experience with an *Englisch* stranger help her relate to Joy?

14. Wayne was haunted by his lack of courage during the crash that injured Rhonda. He allowed his shame and his fear of exposure to taint his relationship with his brother and his wife. I know two brothers who don't speak to each other. Do you know someone who has had a falling-out with a sibling? What can we do to help their situations?

15. With Christmas just around the corner, what can we do to spread the message first relayed to others by the shepherds in the fields?

COMING NEXT MONTH FROM
Love Inspired®

Available December 17, 2013

HER UNEXPECTED COWBOY
Cowboys of Sunrise Ranch
Debra Clopton

Determined never to fall in love, the last thing Rowdy McDermott expects is for spunky artist Lucy Calvert to literally land in his arms and into his heart.

BAYOU SWEETHEART
Lenora Worth

A troubled past has hardened millionaire Tomas Delacorte, but when he hires the bubbly Callie Moreau as his landscaper, she'll show him a world full of light and love.

HIS IDEAL MATCH
Chatam House
Arlene James

Widow Carissa Hopper thinks Phillip Chatam is bad news, but when the charming adventurer starts growing roots, can she trust that he'll stick around for her and her children?

THE FIREFIGHTER'S NEW FAMILY
Gail Gaymer Martin

Firefighter Devon Murphy risks his life daily, but when he starts to fall for widow Ashley Kern and her adorable son, he's not sure he can place his heart in the same danger.

THE RANCHER'S SECRET SON
Betsy St. Amant

Emma Shaver has kept their son a mystery for years, but when she's reunited with Max Ringgold, she'll realize she can't keep her secrets—or her heart—hidden any longer.

SEASON OF REDEMPTION
Jenna Mindel

Working together on a community project will teach Ryan Marsh and Kellie Cavanaugh that sometimes the path to healing can also be the path to love.

LICNM1213

REQUEST YOUR FREE BOOKS!

2 FREE INSPIRATIONAL NOVELS
PLUS 2
FREE
MYSTERY GIFTS

Love Inspired

YES! Please send me 2 FREE Love Inspired® novels and my 2 FREE mystery gifts (gifts are worth about $10). After receiving them, if I don't wish to receive any more books, I can return the shipping statement marked "cancel." If I don't cancel, I will receive 6 brand-new novels every month and be billed just $4.74 per book in the U.S. or $5.24 per book in Canada. That's a saving of at least 21% off the cover price. It's quite a bargain! Shipping and handling is just 50¢ per book in the U.S. and 75¢ per book in Canada.* I understand that accepting the 2 free books and gifts places me under no obligation to buy anything. I can always return a shipment and cancel at any time. Even if I never buy another book, the two free books and gifts are mine to keep forever.

105/305 IDN F47Y

Name	(PLEASE PRINT)

Address	Apt. #

City	State/Prov.	Zip/Postal Code

Signature (if under 18, a parent or guardian must sign)

Mail to the Harlequin® Reader Service:
IN U.S.A.: P.O. Box 1867, Buffalo, NY 14240-1867
IN CANADA: P.O. Box 609, Fort Erie, Ontario L2A 5X3

**Are you a subscriber to Love Inspired books
and want to receive the larger-print edition?
Call 1-800-873-8635 or visit www.ReaderService.com.**

* Terms and prices subject to change without notice. Prices do not include applicable taxes. Sales tax applicable in N.Y. Canadian residents will be charged applicable taxes. Offer not valid in Quebec. This offer is limited to one order per household. Not valid for current subscribers to Love Inspired books. All orders subject to credit approval. Credit or debit balances in a customer's account(s) may be offset by any other outstanding balance owed by or to the customer. Please allow 4 to 6 weeks for delivery. Offer available while quantities last.

Your Privacy—The Harlequin® Reader Service is committed to protecting your privacy. Our Privacy Policy is available online at www.ReaderService.com or upon request from the Harlequin Reader Service.

We make a portion of our mailing list available to reputable third parties that offer products we believe may interest you. If you prefer that we not exchange your name with third parties, or if you wish to clarify or modify your communication preferences, please visit us at www.ReaderService.com/consumerchoice or write to us at Harlequin Reader Service Preference Service, P.O. Box 9062, Buffalo, NY 14269. Include your complete name and address.

LII3R

A troubled past has hardened millionaire Tomas Delacorte, but when he hires the bubbly Callie Moreau as his landscaper, she'll show him a world full of light and love.

Bayou Sweetheart

by

Lenora Worth

is available January 2014
wherever Love Inspired books are sold.